THE PLUNGE

Crime by Design Book 5

JANE THORNLEY

Riverflow Press

Either we evolve or we die, metaphorically speaking. Maybe the change sweeps into our existence suddenly as the result of a single event, or maybe the transformation evolves gradually in a series of realizations that alter one's inner fabric. In my case, my first clue arrived the day I could no longer cast on my stitches.

Sir Rupert Fox, my sometimes friend, and I were settled into one of his plush gallery salons by the fire. London in February required plenty of creature comforts plus liberal doses of companionship. Though Rupert wasn't quite his talkative self these days, the tea was hot, the cucumber sandwiches delicious, and I was busy counting stitches, which, by the way, I hated. For some reason, I could not lay the proper foundation for my next knitting project, which I took to be a sign.

"Have you heard from Noel and Toby lately?" Rupert inquired. With his lips pursed and reading glasses shoved way down his nose, he looked to be the epitome of the serious knitter tackling an argyle-patterned tie.

"No," I said, not looking up. "Damn!"

Rupert paused, looking across at me. "Damn?"

"I lost my count again."

"Oh, for pity's sake, Phoebe. This must be the tenth time you've tried this afternoon. Shall I lay them on for you?"

"No. Thanks. I'll just start again."

"Very well. In any case, I would have thought you would have gone after them by now," he remarked.

That stopped me. "Gone after them why?"

"Because one is your boyfriend—that term does seem terribly inadequate these days, does it not?—and one is your long-lost brother, obviously."

"And they both left me hanging, so why should I go chasing halfway across the world looking for them yet another time?"

"Phoebe, do stop prevaricating. You have tracked them down before so it's not as if this would be a foreign activity."

I held up my hand. "Right. It's happened once too often, considering that they hide so no one can find them, including me. And I haven't a clue where they are so don't ask."

"You don't?"

"No, of course not." I glanced up from where I had just managed to cast on twenty of the required hundred stitches and met his eyes. "I said I'd tell you the moment I heard something, the same thing I told you the last ten times you've asked." Lifting my needles, I resumed my count, my mind on anything but numbers.

"Don't be testy, Phoebe. I merely ask because I'm concerned for Noel, of course. It's been nearly six weeks since my festive yuletide ball and I haven't heard a word. Usually, I'd receive messages from my sources by now, and thus would be reassured that he escaped Interpol without mishap, at the very least."

"Twenty-four, twenty-five..." I stumbled over my count and gazed over at him, my needles suspended. "Agent Walker would be crowing long before now if any of his Interpol comrades managed to snare him. Besides, if something was wrong, Toby would let me know." Only, Toby remained incommunicado, too. Both my brother and my leading man were partners in crime and thus always bolting from Interpol, which just proves that crime does literally run in my family. "And furthermore, you know why he's made no effort to contact you." I just didn't get why he hadn't contacted me, though it hadn't been the first time.

"I most certainly do not."

"You certainly do, too. He knows that the moment you get some clue as to where he's holed out, you plan to track him down and retrieve that Raphael he whipped out from under your nose at the ball." How Noel had managed to trick a master trickster, I'll never know, but he'd learned from the best.

"Really, Phoebe," Rupert said, letting his project fall to his lap, "that is quite insulting. He did not 'whip it out from under my nose' so much as take advantage of the chaos that ensued after we bested that Arkangelesky scoundrel. Are you implying that I have no care as to what happens to my young friend?"

"You care all right." I grinned. "But you care about that missing Raphael more. It is, after all, worth a fortune, and a coup for any collector who manages to get it in his or her hands. Of course, it doesn't belong to you, not that that sort of thing bothers you much, and Noel is no doubt determined to repatriate it to its proper home."

"I knew it!" He threw up his hands, sending a ball of vivid lime-green yarn scuttling under his chair as if for cover. "You *do* know where he is and you're not telling me! Did he head for Urbino or Rome, or did he have some fool notion that the painting should return to its last known abode in Poland?"

"I *do not* know where he is, believe me. I've been hoping for a word from one of them for weeks, and yes, I'm worried, too. Look, Rupert, do you really think that I'd be hanging around London if I knew where he was?"

That made him think. It made me think, too, because lately I didn't readily have an answer.

"No," he admitted, gazing off into space. "No sane person remains in London in the winter months unless absolutely necessary. I usually dispatch myself to warmer climes this time of year—Sardinia is quite acceptable, as are the Maldives. I prefer my climates dry and sunny. In any case, I digress. We must locate him at once. I have waited long enough, and simply must take action." He stood up. "We must go find him, Phoebe."

I looked up at him. "May I finish my tea first?"

"Pardon me?" He looked down at his cup. "Oh, yes, of course." He sat back down.

"Why do you think he may have gone to Poland?" I asked, picking up my tea. Counting stitches wasn't going to happen that day. "If he wanted to repatriate the painting, wouldn't he head for Italy?" I took a sip. "This is cold."

"What, the trail?"

"No, the tea."

"I shall call for a fresh pot." He was back on his feet again heading for the door where he paused. "And, to answer your question, I suggested Poland because the painting was once in the possession of one Prince Czartoryski, who rescued it from the museum of the same name, and unsuccessfully attempted to sequester it against the Nazis during the war. His lineage still believes the painting belongs to them."

"That wouldn't matter to Noel. He believes absolutely that a work of art, specially something of this importance, belongs in the land of its origin," I said. "Raphael was Italian, so he'll want to return the painting to Italy." My love interest and brother were definitely Robin Hoods of the black market types: steal from the bad, give to the good, but the steal part was an ongoing problem in our relationship. I, for instance, believed the painting should be returned to its last legal owner, but that was just the influence of my early law training.

"My thoughts exactly, but it does help to receive confirmation from a like-minded individual. Noel does have rather romantic notions about such things, but that begs the question: where in Italy? Shall we travel to Urbino or to Rome?"

"We?"

"Yes, *we*, Phoebe. How can I embark upon such an adventure without your company? Why, we are a famous duo now, renown the world over for our skills in hunting down and retrieving stolen artifacts."

To point out that nine times out of ten Sir Rupert Fox stole back all or part of whatever we successfully retrieved, and that we were only famous among the criminal set, was useless. Rupert remained entrenched in the scaffolding of his own rationalization. Maybe we all are, but that's another matter. "Rupert, to go off on this quest with you would be a conflict of interest."

He slapped one hand to his heart. "How so? We both want to locate Noel for different reasons, yet our end is the same: to find the chap and to assure his well-being in every respect. I assure you, Phoebe, I bear no ill will to the lad just because he took advantage of me by slipping that Raphael out from under my nose while I was preoccupied elsewhere. In truth, I admire his initiative, and the very cleverness with which he pulled off that little sleight of hand—truly masterful, I must say, and worthy of my own adeptness at such things. No, I wish only to assure myself that he is all right, given that art thieves must be tracking him down like packs of baying hounds or lone wolves, or whatever the case may be. Neither of us wishes him harmed, correct?"

"Correct." And that much was true for me, but in the case of Sir Rupert Fox, it had to be only half of the story. "But I'm going to have to think about this," I said. "Traveling with you has always been...challenging. Besides, you know Max is going to want to come. Noel is his son, after all."

"Yes, yes, the more, the merrier," Rupert said, clapping his hands together. "We shall have a simply delightful time. I think it's best we start in Rome, don't you? Raphael spent his last years there and got on rather well with the pope. Mind you, Rome is a trifle rainy this time of year, though nothing like London, being much warmer. Nevertheless, I shall pack my rainwear and, of course, bring my hats. Leather is an ideal wardrobe addition for a Mediterranean winter, as well, but I shall bring several good suits, plus a few stylish pairs of boots." He swung around. "Now where is Evan? I must gather the forces and organize our travels at once."

Needless to say, the tea was forgotten. I returned to the fire and fumbled around with my stitches while Rupert fussed. Admittedly, my heart was a mess. I loved Noel and yet nothing about our relationship was straightforward. Both he and my brother were criminals on the run and here I was once again waiting for a message from them. Always either waiting or reacting, I lived in a knee-jerk state most of the time and yet somehow had managed to continue like this for years.

At 4:00 p.m., I enjoyed a ride home by Rupert's chauffeur, body-guard, and part-time chef, Evan. Evan, a former MI6 agent, had been an endless source of fascination for me since day one. I'd never known a man to wear a head bandage with such aplomb, or to drive a car with such precision. While Noel was off my horizon, Evan provided a harm-less bit of flirtation.

As we wove through the London streets, I met his fine eyes in the rearview mirror. "I forgot to mention how much I loved those apps you installed on my cell phone a couple of months ago—the sock app, in particular," I told him. "Brilliant."

He grinned, and let me just say that, as grins go, his was spectacu-lar. "Thank you, madam."

"My only complaint, though it's more of a comment than a criti-cism, is that the delay between my pressing the sock icon and the explosion was too long."

"If ever we have need to deploy such measures again, I assure you I will remedy that."

Only, it was my hope that I'd never again be called on to knit another sock, let alone ignite the person wearing one.

❧

THE SUN HADN'T BEEN SEEN IN LONDON FOR DAYS, AND BY THE TIME I arrived back at the gallery later that afternoon, there was nothing left in the sky but a blur of dark gray sprinkled by flurries. Baker & Mermaid's rich patterned carpets glowed like an island of warmth and color as I entered the glass door, and not for the first time I flushed with gratitude to my godfather for giving me half of the business. Since leaving Nova Scotia, my life had become considerably more eventful, if emotionally and legally ensnarled, and seething in contradictions.

Serena, our manager, today swathed in a rose-patterned vintage dress and wafting eau de roses, was busy straightening up the other-wise empty gallery while strains of "Love Is a Many Splendored Thing" played softly in the background. I slipped up behind her and gave her a quick hug, which startled her only for an instant before she smiled. "You scared me," she said. "I am just about to go home."

I held her gaze just long enough for her to read the question there.

"I am sorry, but no, nothing again," she said. "The mail came but only bills and more invitations to carpet fairs. No postcards. It worries you, yes?"

"Yes," I admitted. In fact, I hadn't shared even a fraction of my anxiety to Rupert, but Serena knew. And Max. "The last time I heard from Toby was a Christmas card from Alaska, and I know he wasn't really in Alaska in December, so where is he, where are *they*?"

"You will hear soon," my friend said with assurance. Serena took optimism seriously.

"I hope you're right. Where's Max?"

"In his office doing books. I say I help, but no." She shrugged. "He does not want my help."

"Give him more time. A broken heart is hard to mend." My friend had been nurturing a crush on my handsome godfather for months now, but he had no idea. In truth, he had yet to get over my pseudo-aunt's treachery, though it had been years since I helped put Maggie behind bars.

I blew Serena a kiss, and dashed up our glass staircase with my coat tucked under my arm, and in seconds arrived at my godfather and business partner's office. He looked up as I dropped my knitting bag and coat into the chair across from him.

"Don't tell me: Sir Foxy just revealed his latest collection of Grecian gold laurels and tried to convince you that he picked them up on eBay?"

I sighed. "Worse. Now he wants to track down Noel in Italy, claims he's worried about him, and wants to make sure he's okay."

Max snorted. "As if. He wants that bloody painting." He leaned back and stared out the darkened window. "I've been expecting this. I've been hoping we'd hear from my boy first or you'd get word from one of them before that weasel tries to track down that painting." Noel, my main squeeze (my only squeeze), was also Max's son. Keep it in the family, I say.

"But we haven't," I pointed out unnecessarily. Plopping my bag on my lap, I sat down. "And Rupert's determined to get that masterpiece if for no other reason than to come out on top. And he says everyone now knows that the Raphael has been found and is hunting Noel. Both he and Toby could be in real danger, and I don't mean from Rupert, who wouldn't actually hurt Noel." I paused. "Would he?"

"Who knows? You didn't see his face after he realized what Noel had done."

"Rupert may be manipulative and conniving but he's not malicious, and no murderer." Still, he had been good to Noel in his twisted way, so he was more than a little hurt over the perceived betrayal, despite his best efforts to hide it. "Anyway, we can't let him go off on this trail without us. We have to do something."

"We do." He leaned over the desk toward me. "Now listen, darlin', you know how dangerous this is going to be, and don't think I haven't already thought about how we can find him. I really expected you'd get a postcard by now." It was usually Noel who made contact since Toby was confined to a wheelchair and thus rarely left wherever those two considered home base.

"So did I." I'm sure Noel had heard me when I said that I'd come to him the next time I received one of his postcards. But then, there had been a lot going on at the time—shootouts, blazing helicopters, an explosion. "Our best option is to go with Rupert. He has contacts all over the world, plus the wealth and means to locate people in ways we can't. Let's play along, pretend that we're helping him when, in fact, we'll be waiting for a chance to beat him to it. Unless Noel or Toby contact us, that's our best hope." And, in truth, I just wanted to get moving.

"It's also as risky as hell."

"So, what isn't?" At that moment a familiar buzzing like a swarm of bees—my ringtone for my "Foxy" phone, the secure phone Rupert had given me—was emanating from my knitting bag. I had the iPhone pressed to my ear in seconds. "Hello?"

"Phoebe, Rupert here. Would you and Max be ready for an 11:00 p.m. pickup tonight? I've devised a route that takes us first to Prague, then to Paris, and on to our ultimate destination, Rome, as a deflection of sorts. Though tedious, it is most prudent that we not fly a direct route since both of us are under surveillance. Still, we must make haste."

I caught Max's eye. "Sure, swing by here at 11:00 to collect our luggage, but Max and I think it's best that we travel separately for the same reasons you mentioned. We need to arrange things here at the gallery first, anyway, so we'll make our own travel plans, and we'll meet you in Rome tomorrow night."

"Ah, yes, that is probably wise. Will you be taking a great deal of luggage?"

"The usual, but we'll be traveling by train for part of the way, so I'd rather not be too encumbered. You travel first class with half your closet in tow so our few added pieces shouldn't be too onerous."

"Very well. We will be by at 11:00 p.m. to collect your things." He clicked off and I turned to Max.

"You sneaky little devil." My godfather grinned. "That's my girl."

"Woman," I said, "Say: *'That's my woman.'*"

My godfather looked at me quizzically. "Wouldn't that make us sound like a couple? It sounds a heck of a lot better my way."

❧ 2 ❧

"**A**re you really going to give that stuff up?" Max stood in the living room of my above-gallery flat gazing down at the cubbyhole under the floorboards where I'd been hiding a stash of Etruscan gold for over two years.

"I really am." I continued carefully spreading the ancient gold—eight single earrings of exquisitely crafted goddesses and beasts, plus a masterpiece of a necklace bearing five tiny shields and scrolls. All were heartbreakingly lovely and no one could have treasured them more than me, but I was just one person and this legacy belonged to all, preferably a museum. "I must. This is my only chance of getting them back to Italy the way they came." Well, sort of the way they came. Technically, I brought them into England secreted in the false bottom of a suitcase Rupert had given me, but since I'd had no idea that they were there, I hold myself blameless. The fact that I did nothing to return them or alert the police for all these months was a different story. "Rupert is going to take them with him to Italy, whether he likes it or not. He owes me."

"Yeah, he does owe you, big-time, darlin', but there's the little matter of the conniving weasel keeping the stuff for himself. I wouldn't put anything past him."

"I'd thought of that, but I doubt he'd want a collection of single earrings. You know Rupert: he prefers his artifacts pristine." On the other hand, that magnificent necklace certainly qualified, and thus required a special caveat. I lifted it carefully, holding it between my fingers so that the lamplight flickered against its surface. "I hate to part with it, especially since it was a gift, but I couldn't live with myself if I kept it." That I'd been living with it just fine for months was beside the point. It needed to return to its rightful home and this was the safest route. "I plan to let Nicolina know that I'm giving it back to her. That way she'll be expecting it. I'll find a way to get in touch with her."

"If you must," Max said. "It certainly isn't doing you any good stuffed under there."

Returning the gold to the pouch, I climbed to my feet, and was about to place the little bag into the suitcase's false bottom when a single earring slipped through the opening and clattered to the floor. It was my goddess earring, the single dangle with the face of a woman staring out in regal mystery above a stream of golden beading. Picking her up, I held her to eye level. "She wants to stay with me."

"My gran would say that was a sign," Max remarked.

"That's because your gran was Irish," I said while returning the earring to my cubbyhole, "and so was mine, so that settles the matter: I'm keeping it."

I flattened the velvet cloth with the rest of the gold into the Vuitton roller bag. According to Rupert, it had been fitted with X-ray-proof lining that could thwart even the most sensitive screening devices. For his sake, I hoped it worked. Either way, I wasn't too concerned. He had been part of the plan to smuggle it in, so he could now be the one to smuggle it out.

"There," I said, layering in more winter clothes. I zipped up the bag and lifted the backpack I planned on accompanying me on our leg of the trip. "Are you all packed?"

"I am," Max said with a satisfied nod. "I have my bag downstairs waiting for Boy Friday to collect while I'll just carry my leather satchel. I just got off the phone with Serena. She's happy to take care of the gallery while we're gone and will tell everyone that we're off on a textile-buying excursion—she suggested textiles rather than carpets to give us the broadest possible latitude. That's one smart girl."

"One smart *woman*."

"That's what I said. Anyway, she'll be ready when that Interpol bludger comes around asking questions."

Sam Walker, who had become like our personal Interpol agent, had resumed interest in our activities following the Raphael debacle. He'd been waiting for us to take off on Noel's trail for weeks, so I had no doubt that he'd be following us no matter what story Serena gave him. Maybe we could stay one step ahead of him.

"So, I booked our tickets," Max continued. "We take the overnighter to Amsterdam, from there fly to Frankfurt, then on to Rome. With a little luck, that should give us a little distance between us and tailgaters."

Max and I had accepted constant surveillance as part of our lives since Noel and Toby had pulled off their first heist years ago. Since then, there was always a crook or two watching us in hopes that we might lead them to treasure somewhere. We never did, of course. The details of where or how Toby and Noel disposed of their artifacts, we never knew. Supposedly, they were repatriated to museums and art galleries, their thefts never being about personal gain so much as protecting priceless artifacts against greedy private collectors and unscrupulous thieves. Or that's what I told myself.

I suspected Rupert held scraps of information deep in his sartorial chest, but I requested that he tell me nothing regarding the specifics. Knowing details made me culpable, not that that made much difference, considering the situations I found myself in. I walked a fine line, a tightrope walker balancing above the moral morass determined not to glance down.

"Damn—I have to phone Brenda to let her know I'll be missing a few self-defense sessions with her."

"No loss," he muttered as he lifted the bag and headed downstairs, leaving me to finish locking up my flat and setting the alarm. He didn't appreciate pushy women and, for some reason, had yet to put me in that category.

I had no cat, no dog—nothing to worry about but the gallery. Traveling at a moment's notice had become so easy. Fact was, I couldn't wait to hit my own *send* button. I'd been hanging on for so long to hear from Noel and Toby that their absence had drilled a hole in my heart large enough for me to wallow in.

Downstairs, the gallery lights had been dimmed, communicating that we were closed—not that we had many carpet shoppers hitting the streets that late. I slipped up to the plate-glass windows and peered out at the London street. "Do you think there's somebody out there watching us?"

Max, who was busy adjusting the Zulu beaded loincloth in one of the center tables, didn't look up. "Across the street, second floor, third window to the right. Bastard's been keeping an eye on us for weeks."

My gaze swerved to the window in question. Though I couldn't see anyone, it felt dark and watchful enough to send a shiver down my back. "Really? Is it the Raphael he wants?"

"Probably. Until now we've attracted mostly bottom-feeders, but the Raphael is bait for a different type of crook. Art thieves are a high-end breed of dropkick but no less murdering bastards."

"Comforting. Still, it could be one of Noel's." He'd put out a "friendly" tail on me before. Unfortunately, they all wound up dead.

"If it was Noel's, he'd have made contact by now. Don't worry, darlin', I intend to pack a gun. I'll acquire one in Italy."

"And that's supposed to make me feel better?" My love/hate relationships with guns hadn't lessened, even though I'd been known to use one on occasion. "What about one of Maggie's?"

"I'm not into the pearl-handled variety, Phoeb. I plan to choose my own."

"A manly version, you mean?"

"A Baretta Executive Elite."

"I rest my case." I would have engaged him on what kind of executive needed his or her own firearm but an inky-black Bentley had just cruised up to the curb. "They've arrived," I said, unlocking the door.

In moments, Evan had bounded up to hold the door for Rupert as his employer swept into the gallery, resplendent in a black leather and gray flannel ensemble brightened by a lime-green brioche scarf. "Good evening, Phoebe, and to you, Max. A very fine night for travel, I'd say.

Are you aware that there's a fellow holed out in an Audi down the street?"

Max strolled forward. "Didn't know about that one," he remarked. "I've spotted a few others keeping us in their sights. We'll have a time of it keeping them off our tail tonight."

I held on to the hope that one of them was from Noel, since he'd be aware of how much danger his latest move put us in.

"We'll draw a few of them away, have no fear," Rupert said, raising a gloved hand. "Evan will give them a merry chase, isn't that so, my boy?" He turned to his right-hand man, now standing by the door scanning the street.

"Indeed, sir." Evan nodded. I knew for a fact that Evan's diversion tactics were suitably spy-worthy. I'd been a passenger on a few rides that had gouged my memory.

"We've already changed our departure location from Heathrow to London City airport to throw them off our scent. Won't this be fun? Quite like old times, wouldn't you say, old chap?" Rupert said, turning to Max.

"Not quite," Max said. "This time it's all about assuring my boy's safety, not lining our pockets."

Rupert turned away. "Just so, just so. Nevertheless, surely you will enjoy a spot of excitement after so long a sojourn? It is that to which I refer."

"Oh, Max, admit it," I interrupted. "You love the stimulation of traveling again. It's been years."

"Too long," he said brusquely.

Though I doubted Rupert was alluding to Max's bout with alcoholism and his subsequent detox stint, it was a touchy subject well worth avoiding. Their recent truce was delicate, at best. "Well, then," I continued, "let's get on with it. Rupert, here's the luggage we'd like you to take for us—thanks for that, by the way. Max and I will make better time traveling light."

Rupert gazed down at the two bags, mine the uncharacteristically classy Vuitton and Max's a battered old-school suitcase. "Is that not one of those I presented you? Surely you will be taking more than that? We may be gone for weeks."

"If I need anything else, I'll buy it. And because I'm one of those honest types, I'll tell you up front that the gold you packed into that same bag two years ago is right back inside the false bottom. You're going to transport it to Italy with the rest of your stuff."

"I am?"

"You are, and don't think you can slither your way out of it."

"Slither? Phoebe, you insult me. I do not slither—"

"You bloody well do," Max interjected. "You're worse than one of those monster snails—a giant sleeze-bag escargot. I—"

"Sir Rupert," Evan said as he swung away from the window. "The gold will be perfectly safe with us. I need only add a layer of that screening fiber I developed to further guard the contents. Luckily I brought extra."

Rupert looked from his bodyguard and back to me. "Very well," he sighed. "But I know Nicolina will be most disappointed to learn that you are returning her gift, the gold being her measure of gratitude for your role in repatriating her inheritance. Giving it back it is so terribly gauche." •

"Oh, well." I shrugged. "I'm a fisherman's daughter, after all. Gauche is perfectly understandable. I'd like to return it to her personally so I can explain why."

"That, at least, shall be easy for we shall be her guests in Rome. Evan, please do give Phoebe the address."

Evan jotted down something on the back of a business card and passed it to me. In seconds I was gazing down at his bold script. "Piazza Sonnino?"

"Yes, her flat is in the Trastevere area. Do you know Trastevere, the thirteenth rion of Rome? Its territory once belonged to the Etruscans, which I am quite certain is the reason why Nicolina positioned her Roman center amid its twisting streets. I would have preferred something airier, perhaps a villa on one of the surrounding hills, but who am I to say? I suppose a countess is permitted her little eccentricities. We shall meet you there upon the morrow, in any case. For now, we shall make haste. Evan, dear boy?"

The dear boy, who was anything but, smoothly lifted the bags and strode out the door toward the waiting car. Rupert turned to me. "Do be careful, Phoebe. Max, I shall leave her in your capable hands. Meanwhile, I shall stay in touch via our special phone, Phoebe. Until tomorrow, *arrivederci*."

In seconds, they were gone. Max and I stood side by side watching the Bentley pull away into the night. "Listening to that little rat go on and on is going to drive me bonkers. I forgot how peaceful life has been since we stopped talking."

"But you'll manage just fine, especially if Noel's life depends on it."

"Exactly," he said between clenched teeth.

"My biggest worry is getting away without those spies following us."

"Don't fret about that, darlin'. Only when we get closer to finding Noel will they become a problem."

We arrived in Rome late the next night after a circuitous route that could have left Google Maps baffled. Since I'd left the planning to Max, I barely paid attention to the trains, ferries, and planes we took in order to shake our pursuers. I simply found a seat on each conveyance, curled up, and tried to sleep, which didn't happen. Nine times out of ten, I tried to knit instead. My project was a bit of a haphazard mess but I didn't care. And if we were being followed, I didn't care there, either. Tailers had become part of my existence and maybe one of them could be friendly.

Finally, we navigated the winding city streets in a cab while I gazed through the window trying to glom on to everything Italian. I did love that country, its culture.

"Here is fine, no?" the driver said as we slid down the narrow alley.

"Is this the Piazza Sonnino?" I asked. All I could see were old stone walls rising up on either side.

"Next block. No way in, very tight."

"This is fine," Max told him.

I left him to pay the driver while I climbed out and studied the surroundings. Tall stucco walls rose all around—houses with balconies, shuttered windows, and garage doors big enough to accommodate a horse and carriage, or maybe an entire cavalry—huddled down over the cobbled lane. The lamps fixed here and there cast a halfhearted light onto the surroundings as if hesitant to shine too strongly on this ancient thoroughfare.

"Well," I said as Max strolled up to me. "Where do you suppose Piazza Sonnino 25 is?"

"Beats me. Let's head down to the next block and take a look."

Only, technically there wasn't a "next block," only a maze of more winding streets dipping in and out of archways trailing with ivy. Occasionally, we'd pass pedestrians with their collars up trotting off somewhere, eyes on the street.

It was late, chilly, and dark, so no one lingered. A clock boomed eleven o'clock from somewhere. Finally, after doubling back on ourselves twice, I pulled out my Foxy phone and texted: *We're here on the streets somewhere lost.* I could have pulled up a Google map but this was so much quicker.

A message came back within seconds. *Stay where you are.* I turned to Max. "He's got a tracking device on this phone so he can pinpoint our location in seconds."

"And that doesn't bother you?" he asked.

"Of course it bothers me, but right now it suits our purposes."

Two minutes later a recognizable figure bounded toward us.

"What took you so long?" my godfather asked.

"Evan, thanks for coming out to fetch us," I said. "We just kept going around in circles."

"No problem, madam. My pleasure, as always. May I take your bag?"

I passed him my backpack but kept my carpetbag close, while Max hefted his own bag over his shoulder in a manly display of self-sufficiency. Despite my frustrations with the power plays of men, I admit to taking comfort in the company of two big ones that night. Though I could take care of myself, at that moment I was so weary I only yearned the safety of a comfy bed and a good night's sleep.

We trotted along behind Evan as he led us through the maze of old streets, under archways, past venerable buildings that counted their ages in centuries, until we entered a spacious piazza. Majestic buildings soared around a fountain while a colonnaded church complete with a tall clock tower loomed at one end. Though at first glance it looked as though every street led to this destination, it still struck me as the best-hidden piazza I'd ever failed to find.

Evan strode toward the church and for one moment I thought we might be taken to a nunnery, but he swerved to the left and delivered us to a four-story building where the shuttered windows stretched up into the dark. I watched closely as he tapped in a code next to one of those arched cavalry-sized doors and in seconds the wooden giants were creaking open and we entered a hallway.

"Phoebe! Maxwell! I am so happy to see you!"

I gazed up to where a vision swathed in blue velvet swept down the curving staircase toward us. Nicolina, as lovely as ever with her glossy dark hair swept back from her face, and wafting the scent of neroli, embraced me heartily followed by a battery of air kisses.

"Nicolina!" I embraced her back, shocked by how happy I was to see her after nearly two years. The last time we'd been together had been tense, to say the least. Seeing her so relaxed and happy was a treat, and I really doubted she would drug me this time.

"Nicolina, you look a vision of beauty, as always," Max boomed, stretching out his arms.

Grinning, she left me to embrace Max before urging us upstairs to her rooms. Evan had already dashed ahead.

"This is your apartment?" I asked as we followed her up the stairs. "But it's huge."

"I own the building, yes, but only live on the middle floor. The others I save for my family when they visit Roma. Do you like?"

Like didn't seem a fitting word to describe a palatial Roman flat. Tiled floors, richly patterned walls, plenty of polished antique furniture, and well-worn but comfortable chairs filled all the spaces we passed.

I'd last seen Nicolina at her villa in Amalfi and this apartment seemed a better-kept version of the same classic style I'd seen at her villa in Amalfi, minus the neutered gods. In fact, I couldn't spot a single painting or statue of a male creature anywhere. Nicolina had a thing about overbearing males, even the mythical kind.

"It's lovely," I told her.

"I am glad you like it. I will have you stay with me on this floor, and, Max, perhaps you would not mind staying upstairs with Rupert?"

Nicola swung around to face Max. Standing in the middle of the marble hall investigating a stunning wall hanging I guessed to be medieval, he straightened immediately. "With Rupert upstairs?"

"Yes, with me, Max," said Rupert. "We shall get along famously, quite our old camaraderie." The man himself had appeared in a maroon paisley silk dressing gown looking pleased with himself and nodded toward my godfather, who resolutely avoided meeting his eye.

Nicolina laughed. "You shall have your own apartments, do not worry, Max, but Phoebe I want all to myself."

"Never fear, Max. I am quite certain you will be as delighted with your rooms as I am with mine," Rupert said. "Would you like a spot of tea before retiring from your long journey?"

"No, thank you. I'm hitting the sack straightaway." Though I knew Max would rather have a toenail ripped off than to be lodged anywhere near Rupert, he was keeping his good humor firmly fixed as an affable guest should. "Thank you for your hospitality, Nicolina. I look forward to seeing you in the morning."

And so Max accompanied Rupert to the upstairs quarters while Nicolina and I stood side by side in her capacious hall. I wasted no time getting something off my mind. "Nicolina, did Rupert give you back the Etruscan gold pieces you so kindly gave me?"

She sighed. "He did, and I apologize for causing you such distress. I did not think. I am forgiven?"

"For giving me a fortune in Etruscan gold? Yes, absolutely. It's just that they are considered smuggled goods and I couldn't with any conscience keep them. I did hang on to one earring as a kind of souvenir, but that's it."

"Do not worry about such things. My fault entirely. I will find another way to thank you."

"There's no need to thank me for anything."

She linked her arm in mine and strolled down the hall. "You have done much for me, you and Rupert—you, in particular. You have changed my life, given me back my inheritance. That is no small thing.

I will repay you somehow, you will see. And now, you must be tired, no? I have left a little sweet wine to help you sleep. Anything you need, just ring the bell and my assistant, Seraphina, will come to help. You will sleep well and tomorrow we talk more, yes?"

"Yes, tomorrow we'll talk." I had few enough female friends, so cozy girl-time suited me just fine, but I still didn't trust Nicolina completely. To be honest, I didn't trust anyone other than Max and Serena, and maybe my brother and Noel—sometimes.

Amid more air kisses and another hug, I nodded and thanked her.

Moments later I stepped into a spacious gold-silk-walled room, opened the windows, threw the shutters wide to let in the air, and gazed around the room. It was as if I'd been dropped into a beyond-five-star hotel complete with a basket of luxe toiletries, snacks, bottled water, and, as my hostess promised, a decanter of sweet wine with crystal goblets.

Memories of my stay in Amalfi came pouring back as I eyed the Santi. The last time I'd sipped that same brew, Nicolina had laced it with a sleeping potion. What are friends for? I sighed, considered taking a bath in the modern air-jet tub in the en-suite bathroom, but ended up brushing my teeth and just falling straight into bed.

❦

I DREAMED OF NOEL. HE WAS SWIMMING UP TO ME IN A WARM turquoise sea—Bermuda, maybe, since that's where we'd met so many years ago. But it didn't seem Bermudian. Too cold. Too noisy. Noel was trying to tell me something, pointing off to the horizon, but why was that bell ringing? *Clang clang clang clang clang.* Then I realized he was drowning and struggled to get to him.

Jolting upward, I stared out into the room, my heart racing. Not in Bermuda but in Rome, with a damp breeze blowing in through the shutters I forgot to latch the night before. Throwing off the covers, I padded over to the window and was just about to pull them closed when my gaze dropped to the pavement below. A figure lurked in the shadow of the building across from mine—a small, dark shape looking up. Though it was too dark to make out his features, I could feel him watching as I stared back. In seconds, he darted down the lanes and was gone.

I pulled away and latched the shutters, my hands stilling on the wood. What if Noel had sent somebody to keep me in his sights? Wouldn't it follow that he might send me a message via that individual the moment he had opportunity? It had happened before. And no way would he approach me while I was anywhere near Rupert. I had to fly solo, and I had to do it now before the others awoke.

In seconds, I had thrown on my jeans and jacket, grabbed my carpetbag and, after tossing my Foxy phone on the bed, slipped out the door. The house was still, almost hollow-feeling, and very dark. I tiptoed down the hall and bolted for the stairs. Soon I had pressed the lock release button and stepped out into the early dawn.

The piazza spread slick with rain, and what few lights still burned in the early dawn pushed pale halos onto the cobbles. Since I wasn't trying to hide, I simply stepped toward the central fountain, climbed the octagonal stairs, and waited, leaning against the stone basin just below what looked to be a marble shell. If someone wanted to catch me, there I was waiting to be caught like a clam for the taking. All I need do was be visible and alone to encourage the messenger to approach. And should he have less than friendly intentions, I was ready for that, too.

It was so still that time of day. No sounds interrupted the steady hum of traffic rising from the waking city or the fountain's tinkling water. The piazza was large enough to host a crowd of thousands, and maybe it had long ago, but now it stood lined with austere-looking villas, some with shops on the ground level, and, of course, the church.

The church stood directly behind me in its porticoed magnificence, and I kept my back to it with some misguided notion that bad things didn't come from the direction of holy ground. In twenty minutes, its gong would announce 5:00 a.m.

I waited and waited, my jacket collar pulled up around my ears. A few figures darted by on the opposite end of the piazza, quickly disappearing into one of the alleys—early-morning workers heading to their posts.

After ten minutes, I felt bored, and then ridiculous. What was I doing standing there in a Roman piazza waiting for a man who had made no effort to contact me in months? Yes, months. The last time we met didn't count since he had only come to steal that damn Raphael. Was I supposed to spend my life hanging on to a string of infrequent encounters, as if that was enough upon which to build a life? I didn't plan to build my existence around any man, so why was I even doing this?

Because of the Raphael. Yes, that had to be it. I had to keep the masterpiece safe from Rupert. And my brother...I needed to see my brother.

Deep into my introspection, I didn't hear the footsteps until the man was almost upon me. I swung around. A small figure lunged in my direction. I kicked out at his lower legs, hurling him down the stairs backward with me leaping after him, aiming for another kick. He landed on his back but quickly rolled onto his feet and sprung for the nearest alley. I bolted after him, determined to get my hands on the little bastard, but he was fast—too fast. It seemed that no sooner had I reached the alley than he disappeared around a corner.

I kept running. The lanes were a tangle of narrow tributaries twisting through the medieval streets. Buildings loomed up on either side. Cobbles, ivy, arches, the occasional small clearing all flashed by. Sometimes there was only one direction to go, sometimes multiple. I didn't so much see him as follow his echoing footsteps, dashing through the alleys without catching sight of him until I suddenly arrived at a large piazza.

Crowded with people setting up tables, some calling greetings to one another, boxes and wagons everywhere, it was like being dropped into a maelstrom of activity. And there I was in the midst of it, craning my neck for the sight of something amiss.

Just by luck, I caught a glimpse of a small dark figure bolting into a doorway on the opposite side of the piazza, and was just about to spring after him when something touched my elbow.

What happened next was pure reflex. I kicked back, pivoted around, and followed up with another kick straight into the groin. I watched in horror as Evan clutched himself and fell back into a cart of oranges.

❦ 4 ❧

"Just stop," I said, exasperated. "I am not some child to be chastised for going outside without my parents' permission."

"Be reasonable, Phoebe. This is not about obtaining permission so much as proceeding with reasonable impunity," huffed Rupert. "I expect you to inform me when you are inclined to take off—"

"I'm not going to inform you of anything unless it suits me."

"Don't be obstinate! You comprehend my meaning. For you to go off alone is simply irresponsible," Rupert continued.

We were sitting in Nicolina's salon, all but Evan and me in night-clothes, the latter somewhat slumped and glowering in the corner. Max was on his feet and pacing while Rupert fumed over the tiny cup of espresso Nicolina had so graciously provided. The countess herself sat aloof and silent, hands clasped in her silken lap.

"I did proceed with impunity and I am not irresponsible," I said carefully, enunciating each word as if one would for a small child or for whom English was a second language. "As I said, I acted on a hunch knowing full well that if matters went south, I could take care of myself, which I did. Whoever he was, he lunged at me and I lunged back. I leveraged a perfect kick to his shin, which sent him hurling backward and immediately on the defensive."

"Kick?" Rupert erupted, scrambling to his feet. "What if he'd had a knife or a firearm? You could have been killed! You know that we are beset by cutthroats and ne'er-do-wells. We are not safe anywhere at the moment. What were you thinking going out there by yourself?"

Max swung around. "Look here, Foxy, if anyone is going to chastise my goddaughter, it will be me, understand? Who do you think you are going on like this, you pompous poodle!" Then to me, he added, "For God's sake, Phoebe, what were you thinking?"

That did it. I jumped to my feet. "What was I thinking? How about that I'm an adult woman fully capable of acting on my own instincts while protecting myself in the process? Listen to yourselves going on and on like a pair of squabbling papa bears. Stop it, both of you. No one's going to chastise me from here on in, get it? I'm not accepting this patriarchal blubbering from anyone." And to Evan, I added. "Sorry about kicking you in the, um, well, for kicking you, Evan. You just took me my surprise, that's all. Next time, knock." I paused, gazing into his penetrating eyes. "That was a joke."

"My apologies for startling you, madam," he said, straightening. "I was merely attempting to protect your interests."

I stepped closer to him, hands on my hips, until I was looking down at him—for me an unusual and surprisingly pleasing change of aspect. "Protect my interests how? I was chasing someone, not the other way around." And now the bastard would be long gone.

"Stop grilling the boy, Phoebe," I heard Rupert say. "You have done him injury enough."

"Oh, I think he'll live," I remarked.

Evan cleared his throat, his eyes holding mine. "Protect your interests by preventing you from doing something you may come to regret, madam. You were rushing headlong into the Campo de' Fiori, an area known for pickpockets and—"

"Tourists?"

He almost cracked a smile. "Exactly," he said. "Visitors bring an influx of unsavory characters."

"Like us." I swung away to address the room. "Discussion over. I'm going to finish getting dressed." And with that I left them to squabble among themselves while I dashed upstairs to my quarters.

I was fuming. To think that I could not make a move anywhere in this city without Foxy tracking me through Evan. How could Max and I ever receive a secret message from Noel under those circumstances?

I stormed into my bedroom. Somehow Evan had discovered my absence and managed to track me as far as the campo, but how was that possible without a tracking device? I'd left my Foxy phone behind for the purpose of providing a signal. There had to be something else.

The room was of the traditional Italianate style—tall ceilings, brocade drapery, lots of dark inlaid wood, all of which made hiding anything far too easy. Even the carvings on the four-poster bed could conceivably secrete a small viewing device. But I wouldn't bother looking there. Though Rupert and his right-hand man were undoubtedly thieves, they were also gentlemen. They would never deign to view me undressing or spy on my personal toilette.

Then I had a thought. Slipping to the door, I eased it open and found exactly what I'd been looking for: a tiny tripwire device tucked into the knob mechanism. Somebody somewhere knew every time I entered or exited the room. Taking my knitting scissors, I snipped the thing in two and tossed it in the garbage. I was about to launch a search for other possible snitch electronics when Max appeared at my door.

"Look, Max, if you've dropped by to continue with the 'bad Phoebe' refrain, drop it. I'm not in the mood," I said, not looking up.

"Is that any way to speak to your old godfather?"

"If my old godfather plans to bleat the same tired refrain, he hasn't heard anything yet."

"Look, darlin', can we at least talk in private?"

"Sure." I took him by the arm and steered him into the bathroom, locking all doors behind us, and turning on the taps as soon as we were sequestered. "Go ahead," I said, turning to him.

"Just tell me what you were *really* thinking going out there to chase some dropkick halfway through Rome?"

I sighed theatrically. "Max, *think*. If Noel is going to get a message to us, it won't be with Rupert and Evan around. I saw that guy hanging out down there and thought it might be from Noel. Why not? He'd done something similar before in Istanbul. I took a chance. And when that guy lunged at me—or I think it was a lunge, but truthfully, I reacted so quickly he may have only been planning to tap me on the shoulder—I kicked out on reflex. Then when he started running, I took off after him. Either he had something to tell me, or he had been sent by another party to tail us. Either way, he had information that I needed to get out of him."

Max stood studying me, glowering actually, with his hands plunged into his terry robe pocket. "By yourself?"

I held up my hand. "Don't start with the poor little babe in the woods routine. I now know how to kick ass and plan to use every new trick in my arsenal to do it. I don't need a team of big men to be with me every time I make a move. Haven't I proved that much by now? Besides," I said, poking his robed chest with my index finger, "the real reason Foxy sics Evan on me is to make sure I don't hear from Noel without his knowing. He's fully aware of the likelihood of that happening. Let's face it, I'm being stalked by friends and enemies alike, and I'm getting frickin' tired of it." It was a testament to my temper that I did not say "frickin'" but something considerably more Anglo-Saxon.

My godfather took all of that in, including my swearing, with considerable composure. Anger management strategies were in full effect. "I understand your point, Phoeb," he began, "but you must understand how alarming I find this in light of the bloody dangers we're facing. Isn't it reasonable for me to worry?"

"Absolutely. Fill your boots. Worry is what we're good at."

"So all I ask is that you remember that we're a team and that I'm not one of the bad bludgers."

"I know that, Max."

"So you could have sent me a text on your other phone—the burner phone Ivan gave you—so I would at least know what's going the hell on."

"I will try to remember next time. However, you have to, in turn, promise not to barrel after me every time. Leave some of this to me, will you? It will take at least two of us to keep our eyes on Rupert and Evan. We can't always stick together. "

He nodded. "Right."

"Great, so that's settled. Now, do you know what Foxy has on the agenda today?"

"He has an appointment with a curator at one of the Vatican museums—can't recall which—to discuss the Raphael, and, of course, I'm going along."

"Excellent. And will he be taking Evan?"

"When does he ever leave Boy Friday behind? Why, what are you thinking?"

"That I want to get back to the campo and visit that door my little man dove into this morning. It's a long shot, but I have to track down every lead. Maybe he was a messenger from Noel, and maybe I scared him off? You can keep an eye on Rupert and Evan while I'm at it—teamwork. I really regret not meeting the curator, but you can fill me in."

"Sure thing," he said, rubbing his face and hair until his thick gray mane stuck out in all directions. My godfather made seventy look sexier than any man I'd ever known, but right then his appearance bordered on leonine. "I'll just go shower and shave. You be careful out there today."

"Of course."

Once he was gone, I began pulling my own wardrobe together. Today, I decided to don the black leather jacket and pants Noel had picked out for me in Orvieto two years ago. The ensemble made me feel badass, fit my curves perfectly, and, okay, I admit, made me feel powerful. I never wore the outfit in London for reasons I had yet to ponder, probably because being a high-end gallery owner required a certain arty air of refinement, which, by the way, I had yet to pull off, anyway.

My clothes were laid out on the bed and I was just about to head for the shower when my door knocked again. If that was Rupert come to lecture me for one thing or another, I just might shut the door politely in his face. But it was Nicolina, now fully dressed in a soft blue woolen pantsuit. "Phoebe, may we speak?"

"Of course." I stepped aside to let her pass.

"Does your room please you?" she asked as she slipped over to the sitting area and settled down into a maroon velvet chair. How she ever managed to look so gorgeous under any circumstance, in any form of apparel, I'd never know. Was it money, upbringing, or just bone structure? Whatever the magic ingredients, I clearly lacked them all.

"How could it not?" I said, taking the seat across from her. "It's all so grand, and your hospitality as gracious as ever. But I'm sorry you had to witness that power play downstairs. The men in my life are always trying to control me in the name of protecting my interests."

Nicolina clasped her perfectly manicured hands. "Ah, yes, as men do, is it not so? I listened to your discussion and I wish to say—"

I jumped to my feet. "Nicolina, I hate to interrupt, but could you just check the leak in my bathtub tap? I'm sure I'm not turning the thing hard enough, that there's some little thing I'm missing. Would you mind? Can you hear that *dripdripdrip* from here?"

She was on her feet in seconds. "Yes, I can. It is a simple thing to fix. I'll show you. That tap, it is so difficult, like a naughty child."

Together we proceeded into the bathroom, turned on both taps, and continued our conversation.

"They spy on you, too?" she asked.

"All the time."

She shook her head, her lovely features hardened into a frown. "As I was to say, you have my full sympathy, Phoebe," she began. "It is you I champion. To go out and demand the answers, without a big boy to help you, that is good, that is very good."

"Thank you, I'm glad you approve." What else could I say? Nicolina had had her own challenges with the men in her life—an overbearing brother, a grandfather who had kept Nicolina's grandmother prisoner in a villa for most of her days, and then there was that bastard of an ex-husband, now moldering in jail, thanks to me.

"But I will go straight for the point, shall I?" she said, gazing at me.

"Please."

"I want to help you. I know that Sir Rupert seeks the missing Raphael, which he believes your Noel may have in his possession."

I was tempted to challenge the "your Noel" part only I rather liked the sound of it. "Go on."

"Rupert, he watches you always, yes? He believes you will assist Noel to reach his ultimate goal."

"His ultimate goal being?"

She gave me a dazzling smile. "You test me, yes?"

"I test you, yes," I said, returning the smile, "So, please continue."

"Your Noel, he is a fascinating man, I think." Her hands flew into the air. "He is not so interested in obtaining this priceless painting for himself, a painting which would easily fetch in the multiple millions of euros—maybe more, much more. It is irreplaceable, a missing masterpiece by one of Italy's celebrated Renaissance masters. But no, he wishes to see it repatriated to Italy before it disappears into a private collection forever. I like this man, though I have not met him. He is honorable, I think." One palm landed over her heart.

Honorable for a thief. "Whereas Rupert is...?" I prompted.

"Whereas Rupert is a delightful scoundrel, is it not so?" She touched my arm. "I like him, I admit. You like him also, yes? He has been very helpful to me in the past, and I have rewarded him generously for his assistance. That is done."

"And yet he believes you owe him?"

"He does. He wants to use me to—how do you say? Reach Noel first?"

"Intercept?"

"Yes, intercept. He wishes to intercept Noel before he can deliver the painting to a museum—likely the Vatican he is thinking, and believes that I will help him find a private buyer among my many wealthy friends rather than see the painting be returned to the people." She straightened, her face hardening. "He does not know me. Now that I have regained my inheritance, money has no hold. I am Italian first. That painting belongs with my people. I am on your side, Phoebe. Let me help you."

I have made many errors in judgment in the past—believed someone to be telling the truth when they were plotting my demise—and yet I believed Nicolina now, or at least partly. But I had to clear up a few things before going forward. "Look, Nicolina, you can't expect me to trust you after that debacle at Amalfi," I said. "You drugged me."

"But we have talked of this!" Her hands flew in the air. "You were very upset, yes—I understand this—but I was, ah, how do you say? Distraught. Yes, I was distraught, and thinking only of my *nonna*. I did such a thing to keep you safe, too, for the Camorra would kill you all, if you were to know the truth. But I underestimated you. I will not make the same mistake again. You are my hero, Phoebe." The hand once again landed over her heart. "You saved my grandmama and rescued my heritage. For you, I owe allegiance, not to Sir Rupert. Sir Rupert cannot be trusted, but it is you and your Noel who will return this painting to my people. I stand with you."

Wow. I stared up into her beautiful blue eyes. A countess was standing by me, really? Besides, whether I trusted her or not, I needed her help now. "Well, okay, then. The first thing I want to do is track down that guy in the piazza this morning."

"And I will come. It is good to have someone who speaks Italian, yes?"

"Definitely," I said. "And the second thing—really the whole reason we're even here—is to keep Rupert from finding Noel, and thus the Raphael. That means he must be kept occupied while I try to find Noel my own way. And somehow we must stop him if he gets a lead before we do. That incident this morning only proves what a pain he can be."

Nicolina lifted her chin. "This I think of already. I have arranged a meeting with Sir Rupert with my friend, once a curator at the Vatican, this afternoon at 2:00. Rupert will ask my friend many things: has anyone approached him? Has he heard that a museum in Rome may be preparing to receive such a masterpiece? Also, he will ask many things about Raphael. My friend will have much to say on all these matters but—" she smiled "—all except the history of Raphael will be lies."

"Lies?"

"False leads, yes?"

"As in wild-goose chase?"

"Yes, that, as well. Let him chase wild gooses and waste time. This man knows nothing of the painting but will talk very much, almost as much as Sir Rupert. He will keep Sir Rupert very busy, and invite him to supper tonight for more secrets. I have arranged everything."

"Really? That's brilliant!"

Nicolina smiled. "That is only part: tonight you and I will meet with another person, very knowledgeable. He will help us decide which museum Noel may try to bring the painting to, but he knows nothing of why you are here. I have said that you are writing a novel based on Raphael's life."

I grinned. "Clever. The fewer people know why we're here, the better, and I can fudge being a novelist easily enough. All I have to do is act vaguely interested in everything." I admit, I was impressed, even a little shocked. Nicolina had taken a great deal of initiative to sidestep Rupert, and had assumed I would go along with the ride, which I would. For now.

After breakfast, we all retired to the main salon to finish our coffees and discuss the day's plans, something I understood to be a kind of ritual in Nicolina's household. Days were not to be rushed but to be eased into with a sense of grace, Italian-style. Max embraced the concept with his charm turned to overdrive as he sat next to Nicolina and entertained her with stories from his Australian days. A beautiful woman, fine coffee—I knew he would be in his element. Evan was not in sight.

Rupert and I, on the other hand, immediately picked up our respective knitting projects, an act which to me was as fortifying as a dose of morning supplements and better than coffee. With the stitches finally laid on to the needles, I could at last knit a few rows, and lay a calm foundation for my day. For me, knitting was all about relaxation and creative expression, whereas Rupert preferred to tackle the art as a kind of challenge to his power of logic.

Today he was undertaking another pair of his beloved argyle socks in the hues of neon pink and burnt toast. A graph he had sketched in a small notebook lay open on the stool before him. At first glance, he could be mistaken as an ordinary middle-aged man with a penchant for a venerable art. Oh, but he was so much more, most of it underhanded.

"Phoebe," he began, without looking up. "I trust you have recovered from your little episode this morning?"

"Actually," I said, also without taking my attention from the needles. I was on my second row and just about to add another color, the project looking as confused as a textile in a threshing machine.

"I've forgotten all about it. Oh, look, the rain cleared," I added, turning toward the tall windows, now thrown open and washed in sunshine. "What are your plans today?"

"Hasn't Max yet informed you? We have an appointment in the afternoon, one which may help our cause, or at least so I hope, as the gentleman in question was once a curator at the Vatican, and very erudite in the life and times of Raphael. There is an excellent possibility that Noel will attempt to return the painting to the Vatican, since that was at one point Raphael's major benefactor."

"You're going to the Vatican? Oh, I've always wanted to see the treasures there," I said with maybe a bit too much enthusiasm.

"Actually, no, the gentleman thought it best we not meet at the Vatican proper, given the nature of our conversation, and, hence, we shall meet at his apartments near the Piazza Navona." He gazed at me over his spectacles. "You will enjoy the Piazza Navona, Phoebe, seeing as it was once a Roman stadium but has now become well-populated by lovely cafés and restaurants. Perhaps you and Max will join me following our meeting for a stroll before supper? There is a little restaurant near the Spanish Steps that serves the most remarkable burrata and I would be honored if you both were to be my guests. However—and do forgive me for saying this—but your present ensemble is not quite suitable for the occasion. Did you, by chance, bring another outfit?"

"Oh, I'm not coming with you," I said, picking up a simply gorgeous shade of caramel-hued silk. "And this ensemble suits me fine."

"Not coming? But of course you must come. What nonsense is this?"

"Actually," Nicolina interrupted smoothly, "Phoebe and I are to be shopping, yes, Phoebe?"

"Exactly." I flashed her a grin. "I do need a few new things and what better place to buy them than Rome?"

"But the interview—"

"Will get along famously with the just two of us and your Boy Friday, Foxy," Max said, stepping in. "You heard them: the ladies want to shop. That's what ladies do. Who can deny them that?"

I could have kicked him for the shopping remark but I was too busy watching Rupert's face as he toyed with the bait. He gazed from one of us to the other, his expression scrunched. "Nicolina, I am most surprised, as I did believe you might offer me a personal introduction to your friend."

Nicolina brushed away the notion. "This is not needed, Sir Rupert. My friend, he is expecting you, as I said, and too many people would make him uncomfortable, I think. You, Evan, and Max go without Phoebe and me. This is best, yes?"

"This is definitely best," I said. "Think of how crowded it could be in this poor man's flat." Simultaneously, I pictured the spacious halls and grand sitting rooms of the typical well-heeled Italian, and quickly returned my gaze to my knitting.

"Very well, if you insist," Rupert said. I could feel his eyes fixed on me, "but I did rather think that Phoebe, Max, and I were to remain together during our investigation."

"Rupert, I need to go shopping," I said, looking up. "You said I could do with a wardrobe renewal. Besides, what could you possibly glean at this meeting that either you or Max couldn't pass along to me afterward?"

"Oh, all right, then, but perhaps I should request that Evan accompany you?"

"No," Nicolina and I said in unison.

"For heaven's sake, Rupert, can't I even go shopping unaccompanied?" My tone sounded much more cross than I intended but it had the desired effect. "We don't want a man around, get it? We want a girls' afternoon where we can just talk clothes and lingerie." For the record, I can't recall having a single discussion that involved lingerie, but my ridiculous suggestion had the desired effect. It was settled: Nicolina and I would go shopping unattended.

A few hours later, Nicolina and I were strolling the narrow lanes of Trastevere arm in arm, dropping into shops, taking cappuccino in a little café, and otherwise biding our time looking as innocent as possible until we could reasonably assume that Rupert and company were at their meeting. There was always the chance that we were being followed, that Evan had been tasked to keep an eye on our progress despite our ruse. At least we had scrutinized every bit of our belongings before leaving the apartment—no bugs or trackers that we could find. This time I did take the Foxy phone, since to do otherwise would raise his suspicions.

Our last stop before getting to work was lunch. Nicolina selected a tiny restaurant with an unassuming decor situated down a tiny cobbled alley where the servers greeted her the moment she stepped through the door. The day's specials were announced on a chalkboard over the door, and I chose *cacio e pepe* with a salad, which was sublime. By 2:15 Nicolina and I were happily stuffed and threading our way through the streets toward the campo, having left my Foxy phone in the care of Pasquale, the proprietor, who would deliver it to the villa later.

"If he asks, we have forgotten it, yes?"

"Yes," I said, one hand on my stomach, as if that would somehow decrease the girth that I imagined expanding by the moment.

At last the lane broke into the Campo de' Fiori.

"It used to be a field of flowers long ago," Nicolina was saying as we strode across the square. Now the market stalls had been cleared away, though a few flower stands still held dominion in their colorful profusion. "But then it became a meeting place, a horse market, a place to sell the fruits and vegetables. But—" Nicolina pulled me closer, her arm still linked in mine "—it was also a place of execution. Look, there is the statue of Giordano Bruno."

I looked up at the edifice of a robed, hooded man, wrists crossed as if bound, one hand grasping a book. "For heresy?"

"Burned at the stake, yes, a most terrible way to die. He questioned the common beliefs of religion and state, the same thing in those days, yes? I always say a little prayer for Bruno as I walk by. A great thinker, a free thinker."

After giving Bruno a little salute, I wove through the vendors packing up their carts, heading toward the door my little man had darted into earlier that morning. Of course he'd be long gone. I no more expected to find him than I expected to find Giordano Bruno sipping espresso on the top floor, but it was a lead, and I needed leads.

Unlike Rupert, I did not believe that Noel would try to repatriate the Raphael to the Vatican, regardless of the supposedly excellent relationship the artist had had with Pope Julius II during the painter's final years. More likely he would eventually seek a humbler home for what was, after all, presumably the artist's self-portrait. He might try to bring it to Florence, where Raphael spent many years studying his principal teachers, Michelangelo and Leonardo, or even to Siena where he followed the path of the artist Bernardino Pinturicchio. However, I doubted he'd go for either location, since nether figured in Raphael's life quite like the Eternal City. No, it would be here in Rome, but where in Rome? My guess was someplace with a more intimate association with the artist's life.

It's true that I was no expert on Raphael, but I knew a little about Noel. His default position would always be to seek out the smallest, most humble of museums or art galleries, and, in the case of Raphael, a place closer to the painter's heart than his wallet. Nicolina had sent Rupert on a wilder-goose chase than she even knew. But all considerations of where in Rome Noel might take the painting, the bigger issue was *when*.

We had arrived at the little doorway, an unassuming portal wedged in the shadows between two restaurants with outdoor tables as well as indoor seating. Though the air was chill, it made pleasant dining since exterior heaters were warming the diners. Nicolina and I wove between the tables, waving away the hosts' call for us to dine, as we headed for the door. It opened up to five flights of stairs that led to five landings, each with a locked door to the flats and a list of occupants, four names per floor. None of them looked familiar.

On the fifth landing, we leaned against a railing and stared at one another.

"Okay, so this isn't going to take us anywhere," I admitted. "The trail's grown cold by now, anyway, but I still think he must live here or is staying with someone who does."

Nicolina checked her watch. "Shall we ring every bell?"

"And say what? No, we have to see this guy on the street and assume he'll try to contact me again."

"Then we keep looking, yes? We meet with Signor Bartello at 4:30. We must go."

This time we threaded our way through Trastevere straight to the Tiber, crossing the great river by a bridge that passed right over the

island where Rupert had stayed in the hospital two years previously. I
kept my eye out for tailers, as usual, but could detect no one particularly interested in either of us. Nicolina walked at a brisk clip, her high-
heel boots seemingly impervious to either cobblestone or pavement
while I race-walked beside her.

Soon we were crossing the road and entering one of the tall buff-
colored buildings so common in Rome. This one had an elevator and
appeared to be an ordinary office building to the casual observer, but
by the time it reached the top level, it opened into an extraordinary
apartment that claimed the entire floor.

"Countess Nicolina Vanvitelli, I am so pleased to meet you at last,"
a man said, meeting us at the elevator.

"Signor Bartello, the pleasure is mutual," she said, grasping his
hand. A flurry of air kisses followed. "Please do call me Nicolina, and
here I introduce you to my friend, Phoebe McCabe."

Our host, a trim, bespectacled man in jeans and what I thought for
certain was a cashmere sweater—canary yellow, very soft, that would
look gorgeous on any man, especially Rupert, who probably owned
several—led us down an art-lined hall and into his salon where the tall
windows had been thrown open to a large balcony allowing the hum of
Roman traffic in from the streets below.

Before us on the coffee table lay an array of crackers and cheese
with two decanters of port at the ready. I settled for water and squan-
dered a few minutes enjoying the ambience, listening to my two
companions exchange pleasantries in that lovely Italian-lilted English.
Studying the drawings and paintings on the walls passed another few
minutes. While not by the old masters, nevertheless they were all very
fine and probably of the Renaissance period.

"Pardon me, Signor Bartello," I said at last, interrupting a discourse
on the weather, "I see that you have many fine line drawings and paintings in your collection. I'm sure you know every crevice in Rome that
has been in some way touched by Raffaello Sanzio. As you know, I'm
writing a novel on Raphael and I'm particularly interested in his
personal life."

The signore paused, his glass of port midway to his lips, his eyes
widening. For a moment, I was afraid I had just made some huge

faux pas, but then he broke into a grin. "Ah, yes, his love life, perhaps?"

I beamed. "He had a mistress, I understand?"

Signor Bartello set down his glass and lifted his hands into the air, cheeks flushing by the second. "Yes, most true! All the masters had their mistresses or boys—" he gave a quick shrug "—but if such love helped their art, who can protest? Not I."

"And is it true that Raphael died in his mistress's arms?" I asked.

"Oh!" Signor Bartello said, hands flying again. "With Luti, the story goes. It was Good Friday, his thirty-seventh birthday—and they say he had such a night of passion, but does a man die of too much love? I think not. And he did not die in flagrante delicto, for he had time to put his affairs in order. But Raphael was, as they say, hard-living and hard-loving—a passionate man. Other things must have occurred. A virus, perhaps. The age was not the most hygienic, and life expectancy was not long, but this makes a good tale, yes? Will you put it in your book?"

"I'm not sure. It has been told many times before, as I understand, but, as you say, it makes a good story. Where did his mistress live?"

"Ah, a small residence on the Via di Santa Dorotea has been identified as her home."

"Oh," I said, nodding. "I must go see it. Would there be someplace nearby, someplace more modest than the Vatican, let's say, where I could see a few of his works?"

"The Villa Farnesina," Signor Bartello said. "Oh, yes, most perfecto. Luti's house is just around the corner, so this will be easy for you, yes? And the master's *The Triumph of Galatea* is in the ground-floor loggia and I am sure you will enjoy it."

"The Villa Farnesina," I said with a nod. "I will incorporate that into my book, for sure."

"It is in Trastevere," Nicolina added. "We can go now, though it will not be open, but to walk the streets there on our way back home will help you capture the..." She paused, searching for the word.

"Ambience," I suggested, getting to my feet. "Thank you, Signor Bartello. You have been most helpful."

❧

DARK FALLS HARD ON ROMAN JANUARIES WHEN THE SHADOWS GLOM thickly between the old city buildings. The lights in the older sections of Rome were halfhearted at best, more decorative than practical. Except for areas of shops and restaurants, those windy lanes remained dark and charmingly atmospheric—unless you were being stalked.

We had been walking for at least twenty minutes and had just reached a little piazza. A church sat wedged between a wall of buildings directly to my left and Nicolina was striding across the cobbles at her usual brisk clip. I called out to her: "Nicolina, wait. Slow down."

She returned to my side. "But of course. You have interest in the church of San Macuto, yes?" she asked, gazing behind me at the tiny somber edifice rising into the night.

I linked my arm in hers before she went into overdrive again. "No, well, yes, but not this very minute. I have to tell you something, and it may as well be now."

I positioned us so that we stood at the bottom of the five marble steps leading up to the church door. For a few seconds, it was quiet here. "I want you to know that I don't believe that Noel is actually in Rome at the moment. I have a pretty good idea that this villa we heard of tonight may be the museum he'll choose when the time comes, but we really don't need to go there now."

She gazed down at me, our faces a mix of light and shadow. "I do not understand. If you do not think he is in Rome, why have you come?"

"Because Rupert is all fired up about finding him immediately and *he* thinks Noel is here."

"But you do not?"

"No, but we couldn't let Rupert barrel off here without keeping an eye on him, could we? In all the years I've known Noel, he always hides out for a while until the dust settles. For him to come to Rome within months of the heist would be asking for trouble. But that doesn't mean that he isn't trying to contact me. I'm pretty sure he is, in fact. That's why I wanted to track down that little man. He could be a messenger."

"He could also be a killer, yes?" She pulled me closer and whispered. "You have made many enemies in Italy, some on my behalf—the Camorra."

"I've made enemies everywhere, but the Camorra is in Campagna, surely, and not this far north?"

"They are everywhere. Do not forget this. Already I think we are followed this night."

I shot a quick glance back toward the street we had just exited. A man was striding purposefully across the piazza, head down, a phone pressed to his ear. Cars and Vespas lined the square but their owners were nowhere in sight. "But I'm always being followed. I'm used to it," I whispered.

"Do not be so—how do you say? *Complacent*. I am never complacent, especially now. You must be more careful."

I turned back to face her. "I am always careful."

"But why do you think this man will not hurt you?"

"Because he ran. If he was a killer, wouldn't he have fought me, tried to knife me, or something?"

"Allora!" she said with a shrug. "Then we will return to the campo and find him, yes?"

It was that moment that I saw him, a small figure hunched into his jacket darting toward us from across the piazza. I held my breath for a second as if exhaling might make him disappear. It was him. I recognized the jacket, the diminutive build.

I released Nicolina's arm and stepped forward, lifting my hand in a little wave. *"Buona sera,"* I greeted. "Don't be afraid. I won't hurt you. Do you speak English?"

As he approached, I saw his features more clearly—dark-skinned, maybe North African. His face split into a wide grin, teeth gleaming in the streetlight. He was pulling something out of his jacket pocket, and for one horrible second I thought it might be a gun, but no, it was white, the size of a postcard. I knew then that the moment I'd been waiting for had finally arrived.

I ran up to him, my hand reaching out to take the postcard. Just as my fingers touched the paper, something blasted him back onto the cobbles, the card flying into air. Then a brutal force whacked me from behind.

A t first, I couldn't understand what was happening. All I could do was keep asking the man beneath me if he was all right when clearly he wasn't. His eyes were staring sightless at the sky, his mouth was agape.

Nicolina, speaking in Italian, hauled me to my feet. "Come, we must catch him!" she added in English, tugging me across the piazza. "This way!"

"But he's been shot!" I cried. "We can't just leave him."

"We leave him," she whispered harshly. "He is dead. We must catch the killer and get back what he stole."

In seconds, we were hurling across the piazza, Nicolina striding ahead of me as always, me bouncing along behind in a mix of fury and shock. Someone killed my little man! Someone took my message from Noel!

Pedestrians stared at us as we ran past, Nicolina shoving them aside with barely a *"scusa"* as we hurled through the connecting streets. She had someone in her sights but I had no idea who. Once I glimpsed a figure running far in the distance but we never seemed to get close enough to get a good look. We just kept running and running until we broke into a main traffic area—four busy streets zooming around a big floodlit area the size of a football field.

Nicolina bolted across the street, me jogging after her, cars honking and beeping as we narrowly escaped being hit. She was heading right toward a glass and iron railing where I glimpsed a man clambering over just seconds before he dropped over to the other side. And shit, she was climbing over that railing, too, which meant I had to also, even though there were people all around, and wherever we were leaping to was obviously below street level and not open to the public. People were yelling for us to stop. But Nicolina wasn't stopping and neither was I.

I could barely focus on the details as I watched her land on a crumbling wall five feet below, with me following suit, landing with a teeth-jarring jolt. In seconds, I was jumping onto the grass below that, too, and rolling for a second before lunging back to my feet and banging into a hunk of marble. We were in a mass of floodlit Roman ruins, all columns and steps and piles of stone rising in high relief against the shadows.

I'd have gasped had I any breath left. As it was, our fugitive was already no more than a dark shadow darting amid the colonnades and I needed all my air for pursuit.

He didn't expect us to be so dogged, was my guess. Hell, I wasn't expecting us be so dogged, but there we were hunting him down through a narrow gulch between two six-foot hand-hewn walls. Plunged into shadow, I couldn't see one foot before the other so tripped twice, stumbling before righting myself and bounding along, panting like a dog hunting the bones of ancient Rome.

What in hell were we supposed to do when we caught him, if we caught him—throw him to the ground and steal back the postcard? That sounded mildly doable, but when I finally stumbled between two cypress trees into a tiny deeply shadowed clearing shielded from the streets above, it was just in time to see Nicolina pull a gun.

"Nicolina, no!"

But she fired. I heard someone cry out and fall to the ground only a few feet ahead of us.

"Oh, hell, Nicolina!" I cried, dashing forward. There he lay, facedown in the shadows before a tile-roofed doorway, a gun gripped in one hand. "Why did you do that?"

"I had to," she said, nudging the body with her foot. "He was going to shoot me."

"Couldn't you have just wounded him?"

"So he would talk to the police? So they would know everything?"

"Oh, shit: you mean the 'dead men tell no tales' thing?"

"Do you recognize him?" she asked.

"Here, let's turn him over."

I took one arm and she the other as we rolled him onto his back.

"I've never seen him before in my life," I said, running the light from my cell phone over a bald man with the build of a soccer player— lots of blood spreading over his jacket.

"I do not know him, either." In seconds she plunged her hand into his gooey breast pocket and pulled out the card, now covered in blood with a bullet hole straight through it. She passed it to me. "Hide it, *pronto.*"

I shoved it deep beneath my sweater, cringing as the wet coating touched my skin while Nicolina muttered to herself in a mix of English and Italian.

Sirens were already blaring toward us. I could hear men shouting from beyond the tumble of stone. It would take them a few minutes to negotiate the maze to find us—time enough to catch my breath.

"I talk," Nicolina whispered. "You follow my lead."

"I've got to know what you're telling them so we're both on the same page," I said, looking up at her from where I crouched beside the shooter. "We'd better get him back the way he fell." So we hefted the body back to its original position.

"Simple. He took my purse and shot the nice man back there who tried to help, yes?" Nicolina said. "We ran after. He tried to shoot us but I fired first."

"Jeez, Nicolina! Our prints will be all over him now, and look at me covered in blood."

"Here, zip up the jacket."

I zipped up my jacket. "Besides, are you allowed to run around Rome with a gun? The police will have lots of questions. They'll keep drilling us and drilling us. So much of that story doesn't make sense, like since when do two women break into an archaeological site to shoot a purse-snatcher?" Admittedly, I was a bit overexcited—couldn't help myself.

"Hush!" she said, gripping my arm. "Leave it to me. They will accept what I say. You stay quiet."

"Why will they accept what you say—because you're a countess?"

She laughed. Yes, she had just shot a man and now she laughed. "No, because I talk many languages," and she rubbed the fingers of one hand together in a gesture that required no translation.

MAX STOOD HOLDING THE POSTCARD UP TO THE CEILING LIGHT. "The bullet ripped right through the place name, and the photo itself is a mess. I can't read the bloody thing."

"Literally, a bloody thing. Two people died for that postcard," I remarked, not looking up, "and here it's practically useless."

"Are you sure no one else saw it when it was whole?"

"I have no idea. I can only tell you that the two I know of who saw it are dead. Nicolina didn't even glance at it when she plucked it out of the shooter's pocket."

"Can you make anything out?" he asked.

"Nothing, besides that tree and the river, or whatever it is. By the time I stripped down, the blood had seeped right through the paper. I tried wiping it off but you can see how well that turned out." My clothes were ruined, and even if they weren't, there was no way I'd ever want to wear them again, except for maybe the jacket. Nicolina's servant, Seraphina, had whisked them off without a word.

We were in my bedroom where I sat in my bathrobe self-medicating with yarn. I craved a dose of calm after my harrowing few hours and knitting was the only thing that worked. Even the wine that Nicolina had sent up went unattended. Meanwhile, Rupert was downstairs blustering at Nicolina, who I'm certain was holding her own. I was using every delay tactic in my arsenal before descending into the fray.

"And the police didn't search you?" Max pressed.

"No, I said. Whatever Nicolina told them stopped all further questions, not that I could follow Italian. All I know is that Nicolina wrapped them around her proverbial finger faster than you can say *arrivederci*. The captain just listened and nodded and smiled ingratiatingly at her while treating me as if I was some poor brainless tourist who just happened to be involved in a double homicide."

"Yeah, darlin', a beautiful woman has that power," my godfather said with an appreciative sigh.

"Oh, give it a break. Men need to think with their brains instead of their...oh, never mind. It worked, that's the main thing. In my case, the captain almost patted me on the head."

"You have other charms, darlin'," he offered.

I gave him a sour look. "I don't want to be charming, let's get that straight once and for all. I want to be taken seriously without pulling sex into it."

"The exchange between men and women has been going on for thousands of years, Phoebe. You're not going to change it. Besides, Nicolina's approach had the desired effect, right? Why get your knickers in a twist?"

"Okay, okay. I just wish that the same old story between men and women didn't keep replaying itself over and over again. Sometimes idiotic men get what they deserve. Nicolina may be beautiful but she's clearly deadly. And that business with her carrying a gun? No problem. Either she has a license or being a countess is enough. And, Max, that woman can shoot." I rested my needles long enough to sip the wine. There was a glass on hand for Max, as well, but he ignored it. Before the night was over, I just might toss his back, too.

"You told me she shot a cupid between the eyes at twenty feet in Amalfi, which gave me a clue." Max was still studying the postcard.

"Yeah, well, at least the cupid wasn't flitting through an archaeological dig at the time. Anyway, the purse-snatcher story is now the official tale, and should the police discover that the victim was a hit man, well, my guess is that it will just get swept under the rug. She bribed him, anyway."

"And Noel's messenger?"

"They'll probably put his death down to some disenfranchised immigrant being at the wrong place at the wrong time. Makes me sick, all this killing, all this dying." Sometimes I thought it would break me. "If I hadn't kicked him down the stairs this morning, he might still be alive."

"You're not to blame, Phoebe. At least you weren't hurt. What if the shooter had hit you along with the messenger?"

"But he didn't. Nicolina had my back. Apparently, as soon as the attacker shot my little man and threw me to the ground, she pulled her gun, and he took off. She's a badass, Max."

"And do you trust her?"

I lifted my gaze then. "To a point. It's like she's pledged herself to me, and says she's determined to help Noel repatriate that Raphael."

"What if he doesn't want any help? And what if she's playing you? It wouldn't be the first time," he pointed out.

"If she was trying to shaft me, why did she hand over the postcard without looking at it? Look, Max, I know it sounds unlikely given what we're used to, but I think she may actually be on our side. Still, we'd better stay cautious."

"Well, good, but how does that help us locate my boy? Are you going to help me decipher this card or not?" He was getting growly again. Spending a day in the company of Rupert did not improve his humor. "All I see is a beach, an overhang of trees, and what looks to be a bloody rope—literally, in this case—dangling from somewhere. Can you make hide or tail of it?"

"In a minute. I've spent an hour on it already. Anyway, how did you get along with the former curator today?"

"He was almost as insufferable as Foxy with his sputtering on and on about Raphael's relationship with the citizens of Rome, as if nobody else could read a damn book on the subject. I've devoured two already." Max took a swig of water.

"Good." Deep into my second row of feather and fan stitch, the tension in my neck had begun to lessen. "The whole thing was a ruse, anyway. The idea was to keep Rupert and Evan busy while Nicolina and I tracked down my poor little man. I'm so sick of people getting murdered over nothing."

"It's not nothing, darlin'. It's over priceless art, remember. People kill for less every day."

"Yeah, they do. Humanity is such a piece of work. Did you lose sight of Evan at any time?"

"Once or twice when he took off to sniff the perimeters—you know how he does—but I suspect he was only trying to stay awake. In any case, he wasn't gone long enough to get his ass back to the other side of the city. You don't really think he would shoot the messenger, do you?"

"Of course not. I just like to know where he is at all times. It's crossed my mind that the shooter could have been a Foxy emissary."

"Never. Believe me, that weasel has no idea what went on tonight. He grilled that erudite encyclopedia-spouter Nicolina set up until the guy was smoking. He even bought us all dinner to further the interrogation, all while you two were chasing after that shooter. Hell." He swung around to look at me, something like wonder crossing his face. "Did you really go scrambling across the Curia of Pompey tonight?"

I pointed to my bruised knee. "I really did, but this is no badge of honor. All I did was scramble after Nicolina. Oh, crud, let me look at the postcard again." Reluctantly, I put aside my knitting and joined Max under the light.

Taking the mangled fragment between my fingers, I studied the photo again, a little magical thinking hoping that the postcard had suddenly manifested fully formed. Of course, it hadn't. It still showed half of a photo—the rest splotched in red and rust-colored grime and perforated in the upper right-hand corner where the description had resided—of what looked to be a bit of sand, a palm tree, and something like a shallow river. "Okay, so white sand, water, and trees—all smeared with blood. Not much to go on."

"It's not all blood," Max said, peering over my shoulder. "In fact, I think some of it is...paint."

"Paint? Why do you think that?"

"Look carefully. Blood seeps, and there is a little of that going on in the far corner, too, but the big smear that runs all the way through the place-name? It's riding the surface like paint. It doesn't wash off. In fact, I can't scratch it off, either. It's bloody enamel, bright red, which is not how dried blood behaves. Furthermore—" and he plucked the card back from me "—see this supposed bullet hole? No bullet hole makes a ragged edge like that. I checked out Nicolina's gun: the bullets are small, lethal little killers, and there's no way one of those would rip anything at close range, even at an angle. It would make a nice, clean hole. No, the bullet went into the bludger's heart, like Nicolina said, and missed the postcard altogether."

I caught my breath. "But that means...?"

"That Noel sent this as a code. He's too damn smart to send anything that would identify his real whereabouts in case it fell into the wrong hands. This is only a clue, part of which I'm guessing tells us that the place he's hiding is bloody dangerous."

"And the rest of the key lies with the people he *wants* to understand it." I gazed up at him. "Like me and you."

"More like just you. He might not even know I'm here." He ran a hand through his thick gray hair.

"Of course he knows, Max. This is for both of us. Between us two, the answer must lie." We stared at one another for a moment. "So, what do we know that we don't think we know? What has he ever told you about someplace tropical, someplace with a rope or a beach?"

There was a knock on the door. Max and I looked at one another before I slid the postcard into the drawer, buried it under a couple of Italian *Vogue* magazines, and strode to the door with my wineglass in hand. Nicolina stood there, luminous in a long deep-red silk dress, looking weary but no less lovely. I stepped aside to let her pass.

"He will, how do you say? Drive me crazy," she said, striding straight for the table to pour herself a goblet of wine. "He asks me to request you to join him in the salon."

"So he can interrogate me, too, no doubt," I remarked, taking my seat and resuming my knitting.

"He's bloody good at that, the cretinous little rodent." Max nodded, his gaze never leaving Nicolina's graceful form. The countess caught his eye and smiled.

"I'm coming down as soon as I finish my row," I said, catching the exchange while simultaneously dropping a stitch. "Shit. Sorry to leave you alone to fend him off."

"That is all right, Phoebe." She smiled, stepping toward me. "The knitting fortifies you, yes?" she asked, admiring the three inches of knitted fabric emerging from my needles. "The colors are extravagantly beautiful. I see such a creation about the shoulders on a winter's day."

I vowed then and there to turn this wrap into a gift for Nicolina. It would look stunning on her, as would absolutely everything else, and probably nothing at all. "Knitting is better than alcohol in my case, since I can regain my composure instead of losing my head."

Nicolina laughed. "You are not good with the drink, my friend. I have seen this, but do not worry, I will watch out for you."

Did I need to be watched by everyone now? Was I that helpless?

"Have you found where Noel has gone?" she asked, taking the seat opposite mine and crossing her legs so that just a tiny bit of satin skin showed. Max's lips paused on his glass. I thought he'd start panting. That was the first time I'd felt a stab of envy, something to which I was not generally prone. To have those long, shapely legs, to be able to run like a gazelle...

"No," I said too sharply. "The postcard is ruined from the bullet and the blood. We're no further ahead."

"I am so sorry," she said, her tone sincere. "I had hoped you would know."

"We studied the damn thing for hours but can't sort out the details," Max said. "Well, except for the—"

"I'm ready to go face Rupert now," I said, leaping to my feet, my project flopping to the floor. "I just have to dress."

My eyes met Nicolina's, who instantly stood up. "I understand. You do not trust me. This is good, Phoebe. Trust no one, that is always best, but this I promise: anything you ask, I will do for you." And with that she strode from the room. "I will await you downstairs," she said before shutting the door.

Max looked at me. "Well, that was bloody rude. She saved your life."

"I said I don't totally trust her, and the fact that she's beautiful and sexy doesn't change a thing. Would you mind waiting for me downstairs?"

❦ 6 ❦

I made some excuse about needing my space while the others were at breakfast the next morning. "My space" actually consisted of Googling photos for the beach+swinging+rope+tropical combinations while nibbling on a roll and sipping coffee. Already I'd found five possibilities, though none of them seemed quite on target. Most had some, but not all, of the criteria. And my mind was not conjuring any dazzling tidbits from conversations between Noel and me that could throw a stronger light on this elusive destination, either.

I was just about to zero in on one of the more promising photos when someone knocked sharply at my door. I flipped the laptop closed and went to answer it. Nicolina's fierce little servant, Seraphina, nearly pushed her way into my room, and shut the door behind her.

"You must stop the search," she said quickly, her short gamin hairstyle and large eyes giving her the appearance of Audrey Hepburn gone rogue. "You must do this now," she said. Just in case I missed the point, she dashed over to my laptop and shut it down.

"Whoa!" I cried. "What's going on?"

"The big lug hacks into our wireless!"

It took me a second to catch on. "Shit! Do you mean Evan?"

She nodded. "Yes, big, handsome lug—him."

"How do you know?"

Her hands flew in the air. "I watch the network always—I protect my mistress and now you. I see that he tries to spy on what you do."

I slapped my forehead. "I should have known. Wait." My brain spun through a thousand possibilities. "Turn it back on. I'll just go back to doing what I was doing, only with different searches."

She caught my drift and smiled. "I see, good."

After she'd left, I Googled museums in Poland and then, just because I felt like it, added in some Italian porn sites for good measure. A few minutes later, I slipped out of the door and headed upstairs, the sound of Max's voice booming from below followed by something like a querulous response from Rupert. Nicolina's patience had to be getting severely tested.

The top floor of Nicolina's town villa was similar to the one below only slightly more masculine—heavier furniture, darker wood. Like our quarters, the walls were hung with tapestries and carpets, only here hunting themes dominated with plenty of Renaissance men riding horses accompanied by packs of braying dogs. It was the first time I'd seen a male portrayed in the entire house, and it struck me as significant that they all appeared to be tracking down something or other. This must be where she always housed the men in her family. Nicolina, it appeared, believed in segregation.

I didn't know which room was Rupert's, but I knew from prior travels that it would likely be the biggest and the best. He would insist. Evan, on the other hand, being the loyal servant, bodyguard, and all-round dogsbody, would room nearby, preferably within earshot. Usually he kept his door open in the event that his master might squeak in alarm and require him to come running.

More than once I'd had the wicked thought that I wished he'd be on call for me. I'd know how to keep him busy. Hell, what was I thinking? I definitely needed to find Noel and soon.

As suspected, the door of a room midway down the hall stood ajar right across the corridor from another I knew must be Rupert's. I knocked briefly and strode inside. The man who had been sitting at his laptop jumped to his feet. Wearing nothing but a pair of striped pajama bottoms—pajama bottoms, really?—he stood bare-chested and obviously shocked to see me as I was to see (so much of im.

"Ah, sorry to interrupt your spying on me. I hope you're enjoying the porn sites. I chose them just for you," I said, allowing my gaze to wander down to southern climes. Abstinence makes the heart grow naughty.

"I, ah..." It was rare for this man to be at a loss for words—as brief as his words usually were—but right then I was too busy admiring the view to notice. That bare expanse of chest smoothed over impressive musculature with biceps that obviously pumped iron when no one was looking. When I finally pulled my gaze back up to his face, I realized he had been watching me study him, his lips quirked in the tiniest smile. "I wasn't expecting you, madam. I apologize for my lack of clothing," he said, rallying at last.

"Don't apologize," I said quickly. "I mean, obviously you didn't know I'd want to come...um, had thought of coming." *Shit.* "What I mean is that I only came to say that I know you've been spying on me and it has to stop—the trip wire on my door, the bugs, and this morning the hacking are just all too much." I stepped forward. "After all, we're supposed to be on the same side."

As if to strengthen my point, I slipped behind the desk until I stood directly in front of him, looking up, way up. The little lip-quirk had intensified. I fought a ridiculous urge to stroke it with my finger.

Here was one of those men who mostly kept his face expression-less. He favored the firm square-jawed crinkly-eyed look of a man biting down hard on a zillion opinions he'd probably never voice. It drove me crazy. I cleared my throat. "Did you hear me? I said I want it to stop."

"I heard you, madam. How exactly do you propose to make it stop?" he asked, gazing down at me.

How did I exactly? Would kissing him help? I tried to pull myself together. "By reminding you that we are on the same team here, and that you spying on us is a total breach of trust. I realize that you're doing it under orders from Rupert and I'll have words with him directly, but in the meantime—" but in the meantime I had to get out of there and fast "—in the meantime, just stop." I turned and strode for the door where I paused. "By the way, I hope I didn't do any lasting damage yesterday morning."

This time he actually grinned. "I assure you that I am in perfect working order in all respects, madam."

I didn't even grasp what he said, I was too entranced by how he said it—that grin, the twinkling eyes. "Just make sure you keep it that way." And then I bolted.

My cheeks flamed all the way to my room where I ran for the bathroom and splashed cold water on my face. Well, hell and damnation, I'd made a mess of that, hadn't I? Minutes later, I descended all the way down, my knitting tucked under my arm, and strode directly into the breakfast room following the sound of raised voices.

Directly in my line of vision sat Nicolina, her hands in her lap, her face rigid with forced patience. She caught my eye and rolled hers to the ceiling before returning her gaze to her two companions.

Rupert was dabbing his lips with a napkin. The breakfast dishes had been cleared but a decanter of coffee sat nearby a floral arrangement. "Max, I implore you to be reasonable. I merely suggest that we remain together at all times in the event Noel attempts to contact one of us and—"

"Foxy, let me make it perfectly clear for the umpteenth time—are you bloody hard of hearing or something?" my godfather said, balling his own napkin in his fist and dropping it onto the tablecloth. "I can no more bear to think of spending every hour of my waking day in your company than I can of having my fingernails pulled out one by one while someone plays rap music in the background—"

"Gentlemen," I said loudly. "That's enough." They all turned to look at me. I took my seat at the table, pulled out my knitting, and began working a tight little row of seed stitch to help ground myself. "Rupert, we have been holding out on you and for that I apologize, but this business of you spying on us only ruins any chance we have of truly working together." I raised my gaze to his. "I just caught Evan hacking into my Google searches. When's it going to end? How can you call me a friend one minute and treat me like an enemy the next?"

"Why, you sneaky little scoundrel," Max began. "I should throttle you—"

"Max." I shot him a warning glance before returning my attention back to Rupert. "Well?"

Rupert's face reddened, giving his head the appearance of a rosy bullfrog perched on a snow-white lily pad. "Phoebe, I merely attempt to keep you safe and—"

"Bullshit!" And to Nicolina I hastily apologized, to which she cast me a brilliant smile. Back to Rupert. "You are afraid we're going to receive information and not share it with you, and that's why you're spying on us—admit it."

Rupert shifted in his seat, dabbed his forehead with a hanky, and sighed. "Very well, I admit that the possibility has crossed my mind, but believe me, Phoebe, I am also concerned for your safety, which is only natural, considering the many situations in which we have found ourselves, so—"

"So, you're going to cease and desist in the interests of our continued collaboration, because if you don't, Max and I will leave right now, making any opportunity for you to discover Noel's whereabouts that much more difficult." I got to my feet. "I want you to give me your word as a gentleman. Your word is still worth something, isn't it?"

"Well, of course it is. What are you implying?" Rupert huffed.

"We won't go there. Give me your word right now that you will immediately stop spying on Max and me, and in exchange I'll offer full disclosure."

Rupert stared at me across the table, his mouth working as if he was sucking on a breath mint. "Very well, I shall promise that if you stop hiding and feeding me falsehoods about the true events of last night, and otherwise insulting my intelligence, I will immediately cease spying on you for this occasion."

"Fine, and in exchange I will hereby lay my cards on the table—well, the only one I've received to date." I plucked out the enigmatic postcard from my knitting bag and laid it in the center of the table. "I received this from Noel yesterday." There was a multiple inhalation of breaths, the sharpest coming from Max.

Rupert leaped to his feet and snatched the card from the table-cloth, nearly tipping over a glass of water in the process. "So this is it!"

he exclaimed, flipping it over. He caught his breath and then added: "But it is illegible!"

"Totally, but that's all right because Max and I understand the clues. For whatever reason, and don't ask me why because I have no idea, Noel has taken the painting to Tahiti, my guess is to wait until the dust dies down."

"Tahiti?" Rupert cried. "But why do you believe this illegible ruined card is from Tahiti?"

"It probably isn't," I said reasonably. "That's not the point. The point is that Noel knew we'd understand the clue."

Rupert looked at me sharply. "Which is?"

"Noel's obsession with the place," Max added smoothly. "He's been crazy over Tahiti ever since he was a boy and first saw *Mutiny on the Bounty.* He even owned the DVD."

"And sometimes he'd sing strains from that old musical, what's it called— lots of singing and dancing on a beach with palm trees in the background, based on the James Michener story? I'd tease him with the 'I'm going to wash that man right out of my hair' song."

"*South Pacific!*" Rupert exclaimed. "Oh, clever, clever boy, and such the romanticist. He'd know that nobody would ever dream that he'd take that painting and go scuttling away to the other end of the earth to some isolated but unequivocally lovely island."

"It took a while for Max and me to figure it out, but finally it came to us. When you think about it, it really makes so much more sense than immediately dashing over here and repatriating the painting to Italy so soon. There must be hundreds of conniving bastards waiting to intercept any move he makes here," I pointed out. I could think of at least one.

"It is positively brilliant!" Rupert said, clapping his hands together. "Let us hope he has taken the necessary measures to guard the master-piece against the ravages of briny air and humidity, but I am most certain he would do so for he is most conscientious regarding conser-vation, is he not?" Rupert tucked the postcard into the pocket of his dressing gown.

"Always," I said with a smile, watching the card disappear. "He's an archaeologist, after all."

"Indeed, now let us make haste. I shall put things into motion immediately. Prepare to leave by the evening," Rupert said on his way to the door. "You will need a new wardrobe, Phoebe. It will be warm down there."

"I'll go shopping today. And don't forget your promise," I called after him.

"I shall attend to matters immediately," he assured me over his shoulder, his voice fading down the hall.

Once he had left, I turned my attention back to my companions. Nicolina was studying me with quickened interest while Max leaned forward shaking his head. "What are you up to, goddaughter mine? Noel hates musicals."

I put a finger to my lips.

"It is all right, Phoebe," Nicolina said. "I told Rupert that I would not tolerate bugs anywhere in my house." She lifted one hand. "They are gone, but perhaps you wish to speak with Max on the balcony?"

My gaze turned to the floor-length shutters thrown open to the morning sunshine. "Thanks, Nicolina."

In moments, Max and I were gripping the wrought-iron railing and gazing down at the piazza. "What the hell's going on, Phoebe? Are we really going to Tahiti?"

"Of course not."

"Then where?"

"I have no idea yet, but we'd better find out fast because we have a plane to catch tonight. Now, let's get shopping."

7

"What are we looking for exactly?" Max asked me as I steered him through the narrow streets near the Spanish Steps. Here, the area had been designated as foot traffic only with plentiful upscale shops to ensure that we could duck somewhere in an instant.

"Clothes," I told him, "something for you and me to wear in tropical climes."

"I know it's a ploy, but hell, Phoebe, do I really need a wardrobe upgrade?" he hissed.

"Max, we are going someplace warm, and unless you're planning on wearing leather on a beach, yes, you really do. So what if we don't know where we're going exactly? We had to escape Rupert's scrutiny and figure out what that postcard is really telling us."

My godfather linked his arm in mine and laughed. "Hell, you had the little rodent spinning back there. He bought the Tahiti story hook, line, and stinker—as in little thieving stinker—but I still can't figure out where in hell my boy's really gone. Maybe somewhere in the Mediterranean? That makes sense—it's close enough."

"Too obvious," I said, studying the long line of shops ahead. "How about Prada, think we can find something in there?"

"Yeah, for the price of a small condo. Keep walking, darlin'."

We kept walking. As the morning deepened, so did the amount of pedestrians clogging the streets. Though I figured we were probably being followed by somebody or multiple somebodies, at least I was confident that none of them were from Rupert. "Think, Max. What in Noel's past involved beaches and palm trees? Is there someplace he told you about as a boy, someplace special?"

"Phoebe, remember Noel grew up in the Australian Outback and I wasn't around for any of it. I only went back to track him down when he was in his late teens after his mother died. That's when I sent him to school in Queensland where there are hundreds of beaches and millions of palm trees. I only saw him on school holidays until he graduated as a full-fledged archaeologist."

"So, you don't remember him telling you anything that might relate to that card?"

Max shook his head. "Don't forget that we didn't have the best relationship. Everything Maggie yelled at me before she tried to shoot me was true: I was a shut-down, arrogant, obsessed-with-myself bastard. Not the best groundwork for a father-son relationship, any more than it was for a male-female partnership."

"Don't start beating yourself up again. That's all in the past, and you've aced it as a godfather since, in my books. Okay, so you were an absentee dad and then treated your son like garbage, but he really should have called you on it before he turned on you with Mags."

"That would have spoiled the surprise. He hid that well for the decade we were working together, didn't he? But I was still a right bastard. Add to that me being a dropkick by doing the 'love 'em and leave 'em' thing with his mom, abandoning her to raise him in poverty until the day she died. Yeah, I don't blame him for seething all those years and then double-crossing me."

"You didn't know she was pregnant," I pointed out, "and yes, you did do some bastardly things, but it's in the past. You made mistakes, so what? You're human."

"You never did horrible things like that, and you're human," he pointed out.

I grinned up at him. "Give me time. Anyway, the point is that it's done, and you've moved on and cleaned up your act. Besides, Noel is a big boy now and it's time to get over it. Plus, you've tried to make it up to him since—educated him in the rare textile and antiquities business—"

"Taught him how to be a crook. Did a damn good job there, didn't I?" Max looked down at me with a sad smile. "He managed to blindside me *and* Rupert."

"All in the name of a higher purpose, which is one of the reasons he won my heart in the end: steal from the bad—sorry to classify you as a baddie but back then you were—and give to the greater good. Got to love it."

We had reached the Piazza di Spagna and the Spanish Steps, our street being one of many leading to that sweeping marble stairway up to the Trinità dei Monti. I stopped long enough to gaze at it, letting the crowd stream around us. "Gorgeous, isn't it?"

"Even more so when it's not plastered with thousands of tourists a day," he said, staring straight ahead. "I don't know if I can ever convince him to give me another chance, Phoebe."

"When we finally find him and he really gets to know who you are now, he'll forgive you. I asked him to give you a chance and he assured me he would. Now, let's move on. We're too exposed here."

He patted my hand and we turned the corner and strode down another street.

"Would he have gone back to Australia?" I asked.

"Too far away from everything. He needs a place he could get in and out of within a day's travel, someplace tucked away but still accessible. Wherever he is, it must be his base camp."

"Tahiti *is* on the way to Australia, but you're right—not practical." I sighed, staring into a shop window. "Though there's more than one island in the Pacific. He needs easy access to Europe and South America, I know."

All the winter collections were presented with leather, boots, and knitwear dominating the layouts. I slowed him down to study a display. "He was always big on pirates," I said. "We've exchanged a few quips about that in our brief times together, especially back in the Bermuda days. I accused him of being one. What if we asked for resort wear?"

"Yeah, pirates. I remember him going off to watch one of those *Pirates of the Caribbean* movies. Resort wear should work, though in a place like this we'd probably end up decked up like refugees from a hedge fund."

I laughed. "Still, a girl should carry a two-thousand-dollar purse to the beach, right? What can you tell me about his mom?"

"She was smitten by Harry B. Used to hum me some of his songs after we...well, just afterward. She had this old CD player that used to crank out his music in the background."

We were standing side by side, gazing at our reflections in another shop window. "What was she like?" I asked, staring unfocused past a velvet coat straight into my godfather's eyes.

"Beautiful, mysterious, mischievous—an artist," he said, gazing back. "She used to do those sand paintings and sell them for a song to dumb shits like me. Literally sold one of them for a song once: made me sing her one of Harry B's songs and let me choose one of her best paintings in exchange. I later sold it for big bucks in Sydney."

"Harry B?"

"Harry Belafonte."

"What song?" I asked.

"Come again?"

"What song did she make you sing?"

"Her favorite. She used to sing it to me all the time. Don't remember the name, but I might recall the words."

"Do you think she may have sung the same song to her son?"

"Sure. I heard him hum it under his breath once or twice."

The street traffic was reflected in the shop window and, just by chance, I caught sight of a guy leaning against the wall across the lane, smoking a cigarette and casting quick glances at us. I tugged Max into the shop. "Come. Let's go shopping."

The store opened up into neatly curated aisles enlivened with riotous color and clothes with excruciatingly expensive detailing, but it was small enough and secure enough that no loiterers would be tolerated. "I love these clothes but where are we?" I never bothered to look at the sign.

Max leaned over and whispered into my ear. "Dolce & Gabbana.

Should I sell my town house now, or wait until we break the bank first?"

I nudged him in the ribs. "Play along." Catching the eye of one of the lean, chic salespeople busily straightening the already impeccable shelves, I approached, dragging Max along. "We're on our way to a resort in Tahiti," I told her. "Could you show me some suitable outfits?"

The woman beamed, glancing at Max knowingly, as if he were my sugar daddy. "But of course."

We were ushered into a plush seating area in the back where the chairs were positioned before an array of floor-to-ceiling mirrors. There we snuggled into the seats while the associates dashed around collecting items for me to try. Max leaned over and sang softly into my ear: "'*I'm sad to say, I'm on my way, won't be back for many a day.*'"

I swung around to stare at him. "Jeez, Max. That sounds like a lament aimed at an exiting lover. She must have known you planned to move on."

"Yeah," he said with a sigh, rubbing his chin. "She wasn't stupid, and I talked about my boat all the time, the way a heartless bastard woos his prey with tales of faraway places. Being way out there in a landlocked desert, she begged me to take her sailing someday, and I said I would."

"Madam?"

I looked up. The saleswoman stood with three assistants, each holding several gorgeous dresses in a pattern of silken hydrangeas over a deep green-leafed background, perfect for redheads. Gasping, I leaped to my feet. "Oh, I love hydrangeas!"

"Oh, cripes," Max muttered behind me.

Moments later, I was modeling a hydrangea-plastered chiffon top over a lace-trimmed skirt, swirling around in a sweep of floral silk as if I belonged in some fantasy tale with me, Phoebe McCabe, in the starring role. "What do you think?"

My godfather broke into a goofy grin. "You look gobsmacking gorgeous, Phoebe, that's what I think. I've never seen you dressed up like that."

"Didn't know I could clean up so well, did you? But then, you have seen me as Queen Elizabeth I."

"Yes, but the farthingale is so not you." He grinned.

"But this is?"

No response but I sensed he had more to say if he thought it prudent. The clerks and I had been having fun backstage in the dressing room, the pair of them getting in on the makeover scene by doing something clever with my hair. I think I was wearing a silk flower behind one ear. Now that I actually had hair again, it worked.

Swirling around, I was just about to force myself down to earth when out walked another associate holding a floral print sundress and a bathing suit patterned after Majolica tile complete with a matching silk caftan. In I went again, indulging in yet another bout of fit-and-flatter.

In the end, it was heart-wrenching to leave all those silken beauties behind, but there was no way I could afford the equivalent of ten thousand dollars' worth of clothes. I did have the associate jot down the specifics of my substantial wish list and assured her that I'd return once I made up my mind (or made my first fortune, whatever came first). After all, I had to preserve my ruse.

Back on the street, I had almost forgotten why I'd come. "Okay," I said, rubbing my eyes as if waking up from a deep dream or perhaps too much wine, "I've just flittered away two hours and still have nothing to wear in the tropics."

"May I suggest buying a pair of flip-flops and a sarong once we arrive in Jamaica?" Max whispered as he steered me through the crowds.

I stopped and looked up at him. He pulled me closer and sang into my ear: *"My heart is down, my head is turning around, I had to leave a little girl in Kingston Town."*

◈

"MAX, ARE YOU SERIOUS—JAMAICA?" I HISSED AS WE HOOFED IT back to Nicolina's.

"It all fits," he whispered back. "Jamaica has been historically a pirate sanctuary for hundreds of years. It's an overnight flight to Europe, and even closer to North and South America. It's an island, and, more importantly, Noel would reasonably expect me to make the connection between that song and the postcard. He knows I'm with you, Phoebe. My boy knows we're trying to find him."

"I know that, but Kingston is a pretty dangerous place these days, isn't it—filled with drug lords and crime wars?"

"Which makes it even more perfect. Noel would want to surround himself with plenty of warriors willing and able to defend his position. He's in a stronghold somewhere in Kingston, which is where we will head."

"That still leaves the little matter of how to get there without Rupert knowing."

The moment we stepped into Nicolina's main hall, we nearly tripped over boxes and bags bearing labels from some of Rome's chicest gentlemen's fashion houses. Rupert himself stood over the lot discussing packing logistics with Evan while Nicolina gazed down upon it all in silence. She brightened the moment she caught sight of us.

"Phoebe, Max, you have returned!" she greeted, walking toward me with her arms stretched front of her. In moments, she had laced her fingers with mine and held my gaze. "You have had success shopping, yes?"

"Yes, total success," I told her. "We found everything we could have possibly hoped for."

"And yet you have nothing to show for your efforts. How is that possible?" Rupert said, stepping forward. "You have no packages, Phoebe."

I released Nicolina's hands and turned to face him, my brain scrambling for a deflection maneuver. Remembering my wish list, I pulled the paper from my pocket and held it before Rupert's eyes long enough for him to register the logo.

"Dolce & Gabbana? Why, Phoebe, I am most impressed," he said, clapping his hands together. "I feared you would scurry to H&M or even Zara, perhaps, but an actual couture house? Well done! But I return to my original query: where are your packages? I'd love to see what you have chosen for our sojourn to the South Pacific."

Nicolina slipped the paper from my hand and clucked her tongue. "Now, Rupert, she is to have them delivered, is that not so, Phoebe?"

"Bloody right it's so," Max said, removing his jacket. "If you think I'm going lug a bunch of boxes halfway across Rome, you're nuts. I suppose you had Boy Friday here be your pack mule, Rupe?"

"I most certainly did not, Maxwell, and don't be so infernally rude. We used a limousine service, as is only proper," Rupert huffed.

"Now, now, do not argue, my friends," Nicolina said as she strode down the hall. "I will just call Dolce & Gabbana to ensure they make the deliveries correctly. These places, they are always mixing things up."

"But—" I turned to stop her.

"Well, Phoebe," Rupert said, drawing my attention back to him. "I have made arrangements for our flights tonight. Evan and I shall proceed from Rome to La Guardia, and then on to San Francisco before catching our flight to Tahiti. For you and Max, we have selected another route, as is only wise, and have arranged for you to proceed—which way is it again, Evan, my boy?"

Evan glanced up from his packing list and replied. "From Rome to Boston, from Boston to Seattle, from Seattle to Hawaii, and then on to Tahiti, sir."

"Just so." Rupert nodded. "It shall be very difficult to trace us all. Your flight leaves at 8:00 p.m. and ours at 9:30. Nevertheless, it shall be a long night of travel and more of the same the next day, for everyone. I have taken the liberty of booking the four of us in at two different resorts that are situated very close to one another, relatively speaking, where we shall await for Noel to contact you further, which he no doubt will. Does this meet with your approval?" he asked me, pointedly ignoring Max.

"The farther away from you I am, the better," Max said as he bounded up the stairs. "I'll just go pack my toothbrush."

I'd have followed him if it wouldn't have looked too obvious. Instead, I faced Rupert squarely and nodded. "That's fine. I'm just nervous, that's all. I mean, we don't know exactly where in Tahiti we're supposed to go."

Rupert waved his hand. "Fear not, my young friend. I suspect that

Noel will attempt to contact you again with further directions once we arrive, hence my precaution of having us reside in different locations. We can't have him bolting because he thinks I'm in attendance, can we?"

"No, we can't—good thinking—but I'm also nervous because I'll be seeing Noel soon, or hope to, and well, it's making me emotional." That was true. The closer I came to tracking down my criminal Robin Hood lover, the more my stomach flipped at the sound of his name. On the other hand, I felt no compunction for tricking Rupert. I owed him one, or possibly ten.

"Now, now, Phoebe," he said, taking my hand. "You will see him soon enough, at which point we will all vacate ourselves so that the two of you have a bit of time alone."

And so that he could steal the painting back. Got it. I retrieved my hand, cast him a tremulous smile, and backed off down the hall. "I'd better check with Nicolina about those deliveries. Catch you later."

"One more thing, Phoebe: I've asked Nicolina to arrange for an early supper. Even though we will be traveling first class, one must ensure that we are suitably fortified, and that all our tea flasks have been properly prepared well in advance. Even tea in first class is appalling, and the milk equally unacceptable. Evan tells me they source it in bulk and who knows what kind of life those cows have lived. It's most disconcerting."

"Right." That's the first time I'd ever thought of sourcing first-class cows for Rupert's excruciatingly picky tastes. Clearly, I was undiscerning.

"And another matter: Evan will provide the documentation within the hour," he said.

Hell, the tickets. I forgot about tickets. "Great. See you later," and I turned and power-walked down the corridor toward the kitchens and dining rooms before he could stop me with more details.

At first, I couldn't see anyone, though I could hear women's voices coming from somewhere. I waved at the chef, Maria, busy chopping vegetables in the kitchen with her assistant, and carried on through to a little hallway where at last I found Nicolina in an office deep in conversation with Seraphina. I stood at the door and knocked.

"Phoebe," Nicolina said, getting to her feet. "Come sit. We are discussing your predicament. Come in, come in. Take a seat, yes?"

Seraphina offered me her seat with a quick smile and made to leave.

"No, Seraphina. You must stay," Nicolina said. "We must know together how we can help Phoebe."

I took the proffered chair while Seraphina lifted a heavy oak tapestry chair from the corner by one hand and dropped it into place beside me. "Yes, Phoebe must tell us."

"I must?" I asked her.

The dark almond eyes widened. "Yes, Miss Phoebe. If we are to help you, you must permit us."

I turned back to Nicolina, who sat across the carved desk with her lovely face propped in her hands.

"You said that you'd do anything to help me, is that still true?" I asked her.

Nicolina dropped her hands and smiled. "Always. I only wait for you to say how."

"Can you get Max and me plane tickets and a pair of false identities within the next two hours?"

Nicolina's smile broke into a brilliant grin. "I can do better than that. I will get you a private plane."

8

"Phoebe, you can't ask Nicolina to do you a huge favor like that and then not trust her with the details," Max whispered. As we huddled together under the awning of my bedroom balcony, a thick mist settled over the Roman dusk.

"But she could be in Rupert's pocket. Supposing everything I say gets back to him?"

"That's just a risk we'll have to take. You've asked her to help us and she said she's willing. How do you expect her to arrange things without telling her the destination?"

I leaned against the railing staring down into the piazza, now empty but for a few pedestrians hurrying by. "Actually, she did say she could organize the flight so that we tell only the pilot directly, who then files the manifest, or whatever. It takes longer apparently, but it's far more secure than if we told her in advance."

"And you think she couldn't find out the destination after the fact?"

"Yeah, she could." I sighed. "But it still seems the safest route."

"But the Fox thinks we're flying on the same airline, is probably planning to accompany us to the airport so that we can get all cozied up in the first-class lounge before seeing us safely to our gate. I tell you,

Phoeb, we need Nicolina for more than just getting us that gourmet plane ride. We have to do some skirting maneuvers to shake Foxy before we even leave this house."

"You're right," I said, pulling up straight. "I have to do a full disclosure with her and hope for the best. Damn."

"Great. I'll just start an argument with the weasel to keep them busy while you talk privately. Rupe gets his knickers in a twist so easily when he's preparing for a trip. Should be fun."

I paused at the entrance to my room. "By the way, what happens when we arrive?"

"We'll figure that out when we get there but, like old Foxy says, Noel has his eye on us. He'll contact us again."

"Let's hope nobody else gets killed first."

We found Rupert and Evan with Nicolina in the main hall. The countess had her arms crossed and was peering down at the trunk Evan was busy securing. Rupert, now dressed in a light tweed travel suit and surrounded by mounds of luggage, was clearly in his element playing the sartorial master of operations.

I avoided glancing at Evan, which was easy since Rupert blocked his view.

"Phoebe!" Rupert said, catching sight of me, his face beaming in delight just seconds before it collapsed in pique. "Why aren't you dressed for our travels? Where's the Dolce & Gabbana in which we have been so anticipating seeing you garbed, not to mention your suitcases? Am I to wait forever to see you enveloped in the grace and style which would so enhance your natural assets?"

"My assets are entirely mine to enhance or not, Rupert." And since I only had a backpack and one roller bag, packing was something I could throw together in minutes. "Besides, I have no intention of wearing designer duds on the plane. I'd spill something or other over something expensive before we even left the ground. No, jeans and a jacket suit me just fine."

"Oh, very well," he huffed. "I shall just have to wait for Tahiti, but that still begs the question of your missing luggage. Max, surely you can assist your goddaughter to carry her bags downstairs rather than require Evan to accommodate every detail? Our limo will arrive within the hour."

Nicolina unfolded her arms and stepped between the men. "Oh, Rupert, how you tease. Phoebe's luggage comes now."

I turned. Down the stairs trudged the small but mighty Seraphina, carrying my roller bag plus one other full-sized suitcase I didn't recognize but figured I had just been gifted. And I didn't have time to comment on any of it.

"What's with you and your Boy Friday, Rupe?" Max bellowed. "Making the little women of the house do everything around here? I took you for a gent, but obviously you're just the same old self-absorbed little scoundrel you always were! Seraphina, are you all right, dear?" he asked in a pantomime of gallantry.

The moment Nicolina's employee reached the bottom of the stairs, she glowered up at him and dropped the largest bag on his foot. That was my cue to catch Nicolina's eye and stroll with her down the corridor, leaving the men to squabble.

"I am sorry for doubting you," I whispered. "I just find it hard to trust, but now I'm going to tell you everything."

Nicolina smiled, drawing me closer. "You do not trust for very good reason but I will not betray you, this I promise."

And so, closeted in her little office moments later, I told her everything, including what we hoped to be the correct destination.

"Jamaica? But that seems very strange," she said, one long finger tapping her chin. "Yet, perhaps very strange is very perfect, yes? I will call the pilot immediately to ready the flight. The plane belongs to a good friend who is very discreet. He owns the fleet. I have traveled with his help many times."

Several minutes and plenty of Italian later, Nicolina had confirmed the arrangements over the phone, assuring me that all would be ready for our departure by 10:30 that night. In the meantime, she explained, she would conspire for Rupert to miss his flight to provide us an extra margin of time. I was to leave that to her and had no doubt that she was up for the challenge.

"This way, you leave for the airport, and by the time Rupert arranges his new flights, presto!" She snapped her fingers. "You will be on your way. But, Phoebe," she said, leaning toward me. "You must take great care. It will be very dangerous wherever your Noel hides, and in Jamaica especially. I have never been there but I have heard. Let me come with you."

I shook my head adamantly. "No, but thank you, and thank you for all your help, hospitality, and the luggage. That should soothe Rupert's suspicions long enough for us to get under way."

"*Allora*, I have packed some little treats and surprises for you." She smiled.

My eyes widened. "Nothing worth a fortune, I hope."

"No, not Etruscan gold, but other things more useful for your enterprise."

"Another false-bottomed suitcase?"

"They are very useful, yes? Rupert has the best. And," she added, getting to her feet, "in case you need me for anything, anytime, all you do is call me. I will come."

"Even the burner phone I plan on taking won't be that secure."

"In your suitcase, the small Vuitton, you will find an item that looks like a little box of mints. These are mints but better. When you open the lid, a device is activated which sends a signal to me. Only then will I know where to find you. Also, you will find another phone."

I nodded. "Thanks again, Nicolina."

"And if you need to contact me, phone Lucas, the concierge, with instructions. He will get the message to me." She handed me a card.

I read aloud. "'The Washing Sands Resort. Lucas Brown, Concierge'?"

"Yes, he is a secure contact. The number, it is on the reverse."

Tucking the card deep in my pocket, I vowed to secret it in the lining of my carpetbag. "You think of everything."

"Never forget that I am on your side, Phoebe. Always."

Shortly afterward, Seraphina drove Max and me to the Fiumicino Airport, leaving Rupert and Evan awaiting their limousine, which, Nicolina assured them, could never accommodate four people plus Rupert's mountains of luggage. Whatever she said, Rupert accepted, which was all that mattered.

Two hours later, Max and I were fastened into our plush leather seats in a small jet, being plied with sustenance offered by our personal steward, Fabio. Trim in his sky-blue uniform, with his faux mohawk platinum hair and the single diamond earring, he in no way resembled the famous cover dude of the same name, but our Fabio was charmingly attentive. We were on a first-name basis in a matter of minutes.

Fabio, it turns out, was Italian-American and had spent most of his youth in Chicago but now was partners with the captain.

"More wine, Phoebe?" he asked, standing there in his trim designer vest and trousers, bottle hovering over my glass.

I waved him away. "One's my limit, Fabio," I said, the wine making me a little too relaxed, and maybe just the tiniest too self-congratulatory. After all, Rupert would soon be heading in the opposite direction. That could only be a good thing.

Max was already asleep, which transpired the moment we were safely settled into our seats—that would be the seats with the fold-down bed and personal entertainment system. Keeping Rupert spinning had exhausted him.

When our plane was cleared for takeoff and we finally hurled into the air, I imagined Rupert being jettisoned further and further away while we flew directly toward my brother and Noel, my Noel. Dreamy with wine, I imagined myself in his arms, him holding me closer, all kinds of naughty things happening afterward. Maybe we'd be aboard Toby's yacht on the blue blue Caribbean sea; maybe there'd be violins, and some cinematographic special effects designed to enhance our reunion. Embellishment was my specialty.

Perhaps Max had considered what would happen after we made landfall, but not I. I was firmly entranced by my imaginings of the reunion with my brother and my lover, all my longings satisfied at last. For the moment, short-term was enough.

The plane flew along for hours, sometimes encountering turbulence, sometimes with uninterrupted bouts of smooth sailing. I knit and slept, in that order, lost in my rumination of all my hopes for a happy outcome safely stowed along with the suitcases.

After supper, I fell into a deep sleep and stayed that way for a long time, stretched out under my blanket as the cabin lights dimmed good-night, seat belts firmly fastened, as Fabio insisted.

The next I knew, I was being jostled awake. I sat up and stared in confusion. Fabio was negotiating the breakfast wagon down the aisle. "Wakey, wakey," he called. "Warm croissants, fresh coffee, and more. Your wish is my command. We'll be landing in Kingston within the hour."

"Already?" I flipped up the window screen and found myself facing a wall of gray. "But where's the Caribbean blue, the sunny skies?"

"A bit overcast below, naturally," Fabio said with a grin as he poured me a cup of coffee. "Milk or sugar?"

"Why naturally?" I asked.

The plane lurched, sending Fabio tipping backward, which he accommodated with a masterful save, and resumed his task as if nothing was amiss.

"What in hell is going on?" Max asked from across the aisle, rousing from his sleep and throwing off the blankets. "Did we hit a speed bump or something?"

"Just a little turbulence, nothing to worry about," Fabio assured him. "Do you take milk or cream in your coffee? Captain Otello is an excellent pilot. He'll have us safely landed in no time at all. And the hurricane isn't due to hit for another two hours, anyway, so nothing to worry about."

"Hurricane?" I gasped. "What hurricane?"

"Hurricane Lothario," Fabio said. "Didn't you know?"

"Obviously we're not up to date on our storm warnings. Why didn't you say something?" Max asked.

Fabio took a step back, or maybe he was thrown back, but quickly regained his balance and continued. "We try not to distress our guests. We were told that you had to get to Jamaica and so we are getting you to Jamaica. Would you prefer a croissant or a Danish?"

"Neither!" Max blustered. "I want to know why the hell we didn't know about a damn hurricane!"

"Max," I said reasonably, "we were coming to Jamaica, anyway, so let's just go with the flow." Another jolt of turbulence forced us to grab our coffees while the plane teetered and tipped. "So, maybe *flow* isn't the best word."

"Go with the flow—excellent idea!" Fabio said, securing the brake on the food wagon. "Besides, Lothario might even be downgraded to a tropical storm by the time he reaches landfall. Would serve him right, don't you think? Croissant, anyone?"

❧ 9 ❧

Igrit my teeth and put my faith in the pilot, plus whatever Higher Force puts the billow in our sails, as the little jet tossed and wavered its way to the ground. It finally made a safe landing in what was, so far, no more than driving rain.

We dashed across the tarmac to wait in the special terminal area to clear customs. The handsome Captain Otello and Fabio joined us, the captain making a point of stepping forward to shake our hands before · resuming the terse phone conversation that had begun the moment we had arrived.

"He wants to get us back in the air ASAP," Fabio explained as he paced the linoleum. "All the planes are trying to get airborne before Lothario hits."

"Don't blame them," Max muttered.

The customs agent arrived after twenty minutes, checked our passports, and proceeded to hurry us along. "Welcome to Jamaica," he said. "Don't wait around now. Take your ride to your hotel." With that we stepped through the doors, waving goodbye to Fabio.

And then we were in the Arrivals hall.

Max and I stood in the sea of jostling people calling out to one another in some version of English we only half understood—families reunited, friends hurrying friends along, drivers from hotels and private limos waving around signs trying to locate their charges. And we were lost, standing with our luggage amid this frenetic sea with no fixed destination, looking for a sign, literally.

A couple of porters came up to offer their services. "I take you to your hotel," one offered. "Best price on island."

"No, thank you, mate, we're waiting for someone," Max told him.

"Bad day for waiting," the porter said. "Storm coming."

"We heard," Max said as the man trundled away.

Over Max's shoulder, cancellation signs reddened the Departures and Arrivals boards. A security officer came by to hurry us along.

"We're waiting for someone," Max said.

"He'd better get here soon," the man replied.

"You're telling me." Max watched the man stride away to hurry a family out the door.

"Maybe we should try to find a hotel?" I suggested as I stared into the thinning crowd.

Only three guys with signs remained, and they were moving through the knots of hangers-on with their placards raised, yelling for their charges. "Mista and de Misses Randolf, where you at?" one called nearby.

"Soon we'll be the last ones standing," I said as I watched Mr. and Mrs. Randolf hurry forward.

It was then that I saw him, bounding across the floor toward us carrying a sign that said only *Welcome to Kingston Town*. I nudged Max, who turned and stared. The guy was big, well-muscled, with dreadlocks halfway down his back, some of which were bunched up under a knitted cap. For a moment I forgot to breathe.

"Hello, dere." The man smiled—lots and lots of white teeth. "Welcome to Kingston Town. I take de bags." Before Max and I could respond, he had whisked up all three bags, balancing the small roller on one shoulder, my big one in one hand, and tucking Max's under one arm, and started loping for the door. Max and I exchanged glances and hurried after him.

Outside, the wind blew horizontally, whipping the pavement as we scrambled after our porter, narrowly missing a honking car. Max threw an arm over my shoulders as we hurled across an emptying parking lot, both of us utterly drenched. Mentally, I thanked my foresight for wrapping my yarn in a plastic bag before shoving it into my tapestry tote. The things we think of in a crisis.

By the time we caught up with the driver, he was busy covering our luggage with garbage bags and strapping them down with bungee cords to the back of his mud-splattered pickup truck.

"You've got to be bloody kidding me!" Max exploded. "This is our ride?"

The guy grinned. "This mi chucky. Get in." He thumbed toward the truck's cab.

Getting in involved squeezing into a two-seater cab with me sitting on the middle hump, legs straddling the stickshift, wedged between the driver and Max. The floor was littered with candy wrappers, paper coffee cups, and a brown bag of something that Max kicked out of the way while the radio blasted reggae at high volume. I turned it down.

"So," I said, the moment the door slammed shut and we were driving through the rain-pummeled lot. "We're Max and Phoebe. What's your name?"

"BigJo," he said, turning the radio back up.

"Just Big Joe?" I said, pitching my voice over the music.

"BigJo," he called back. "Say dat fast—*BiJo*."

I repeated after him the best I could. "No last name?"

"Dat's it," he said.

I promptly gave up on the name thing. "So, where are we going?" A palm frond skidded across the road in front of us. "And how long is it going to take to get there?"

"It dis a lang way but we take shortcut."

"Oh, good," I said. "I like shortcuts."

"Tell us where the hell we're going," Max bellowed, leaning forward to turn down the music, "and keep down the noise this time. Are you deaf?"

Big Joe hissed between his teeth. "Heps me drive. You sit back now. Jesum peeze, man, you nuttin but chobble. If you chobble me, me a guh bax ya."

"And what the hell does that mean? Speak English, will you?" Max said.

I nudged him hard. "I'm guessing that translates into something like 'You're nothing but trouble, and if you keep it up I'll box you.' Anger management time, Max. Rein it in."

Big Joe burst into laughter and slapped the steering wheel. "Dat's right. Phoebe right on, man!"

Max swore under his breath but ceased his grumbling, which left us nothing to do but stare hard ahead as the truck navigated the storm-slicked island.

Big Joe was an impressive driver, maneuvering fallen trees, avoiding stalled cars, and plowing through rain-swollen roads, all while waving cheerfully at people trying to flag him down. "No can stop," he muttered. "See her?" he said, indicating a drenched young woman waving frantically from the side of the road. "Dat mi bess bess free. Oh, yes, I am in chobble now."

"No hitchhikers, you mean?" I asked.

"No hitchhikers." Big Joe nodded. "Only you I drive. You mi business."

I swung around to watch the young woman scramble into the middle of the road giving him the finger. "Yup, you're in trouble now. So, what is it you're supposed to do with us?" I asked, turning back.

"Im a hep you. I take you safe. Now, nah chat to me. I need to think."

"Got you." I sunk back in the seat and tried to relax. Given that it was an uncomfortable ride to begin with, and that I was zooming through a tropical storm to an unknown destination squeezed behind two big surly men, I was hardly in my most Zen state. Yet what choice did I have but to zip my lips and let one concentrate while the other stewed?

Max just sat with his arms crossed staring straight ahead. I knew him well enough to understand that being in this state of total powerlessness was killing him. Our unspoken agreement was never to discuss Noel with anyone—even in front of someone presumably hired by Noel to help us—which left us pitifully little to talk about, given our circumstances.

In other words, it was time to knit. My tapestry bag sat on my lap so all I had to do was pull my unborn wrap from its plastic grocery bag and work a few stitches to calm myself. It's not that I could see exactly, and I had to keep my elbows plastered against my side to avoid prodding my companions, but just the feel of the yarn between my fingers helped. For a few seconds, I almost forgot where I was, though the occasional jolt served as a reminder.

"Phoebe, don't tell me you're knitting," I heard Max mumble.

"I'm knitting," I said between my teeth. "So can it."

And it was getting late in the day—4:45 local time—with no sign of us slowing down. We had passed strings of coastal hotels a while back, that was before we hung a left and threaded along a smaller road that seemed to be climbing steadily upward into the jungle. All signs of accommodation seemed left far behind.

Meanwhile, Big Joe had turned the radio back on, and among the reggae and the pop music, an announcer occasionally came on to provide hurricane updates. Surprisingly, the announcements were in clear accented English rather than in patois, so we had no trouble understanding that the edge of the hurricane was due to make landfall within the hour. *"Stay home,"* Jamaica Jay urged. *"Board your windows, sandbag your doors. A lot of rain expected with high winds."*

"Oh, yeah, tanks, man," Big Joe mumbled, switching the radio off. "Dere, now. We don't be needin' dat."

"Shouldn't we find a place to stay for the night?" I ventured. "I mean, it's only going to get worse and it will be dark soon."

"What, you be seein' some nice place to flop?" our driver said, one hand sweeping before the windshield. "We stay in mountains. We drive now. Safer dat way."

"Are you crazy?" Max erupted. "How is driving in the dark on a mountain road during a hurricane in any way safer?"

"Dey don't follow us dere, man, get dat? Nobody follow."

"Who the hell would follow us, anyway?" Max asked. "We shook our tails a long time ago, at least for the short-term."

"Ah," Big Joe said with a hiss. "Here, dey all chase de Captain, all de time."

"The Captain?" Max and I said more or less in unison. "Who the hell is the Captain?" my godfather asked.

"He who you come see, man!"

Max and I looked at one another. "Drop it, Max," I whispered. "We've come to see the Captain, get it?" I turned away to frantically knit another row, which in the gloom was getting increasingly more challenging. "So, does this Captain live in the mountains?"

Big Joe barked out a laugh. "Dat's crazy, man! Captains, dey live by de sea."

"Yeah, of course, but we're not by the sea," I said, painfully pointing out the obvious. "Evidently, we're still a long way away from the Captain, so where are we going to spend the night?"

"Up ahead we meet mi free, I say. She hep us. Now, no more chat."

I fumbled around in my bag for another yarn, going by feel rather than sight—everything looked the same shade of gloom—taking consolation in somebody up ahead helping us. If we got that far, that is.

An hour later and we had been steadily climbing as sheets of water streamed down the road around us. The trees whipped overhead as the wind howled, and dusk didn't so much descend as drop over the truck in a blur of swaying fronds and rain-streaked dark. We could hardly see one yard ahead of us. And then the first clap of thunder nearly shook us off the road.

"Hole still, mi chucky!" Big Joe cried, patting the dashboard.

"That was close," I said.

A bolt of lightning shot across the sky, briefly illuminating a fallen tree dead ahead.

"Jesum! Must move dat ting!" the driver cried as he brought the truck to a halt. "You hep me move," he thumbed at Max.

"Yeah, yeah. Let's go, then." The two men climbed out of the truck. Little women were apparently unable to assist big men with heavy work. Leave it to them, then. I calmed myself by picking out yarn by the light of the dashboard.

The next big bolt forced me to drop a stitch, prompting me to give up long enough to watch the men heft the tree to one side. The headlights picked out the river of water streaming around their legs down the mountain road.

"How far is your friend's?" I asked Big Joe once the men were back inside.

"Up dere," he told me, inching the vehicle along the treacherous road.

"Yeah, but where's 'up dere'?"

"Dunno. No can see nuttin' ahead." He brought the truck to a stop again, leaving the three of us to stare through the windshield at a mass of tangled darkness as the wipers swished frantically. Another jagged bolt ripped overhead, illuminating a terrifying tangle of fallen jungle.

"How well do you know this frigging road?" Max asked.

"Well 'nuff," our driver said. "Well 'nuff to know dat drop over dere go way down."

"Shit."

"That's it!" I said, shoving my knitting back into my bag. "Let's get the hell out of here!"

"We're trying to, Phoebe," Max said. "Staying in the truck will be safer than getting out of it, should lightning strike, but let's pull over."

"Pull over where, man?" Big Joe cried. "Over de edge or into de woods?"

And then a horrendous zap shot overhead, cracking the sky open as something crashed down onto our heads.

✺ 10 ✺

I opened my eyes—a concrete floor, puddles everywhere, tangled clothes and luggage, plus a pair of brown legs stretched out inches before my face. I quickly closed my eyes and tried to force away the nightmare. There was a steady drip-drip coming from somewhere, plus the strong scent of damp bodies and...coffee. The latter urged me upright.

I stared and blinked, seeing absolutely nothing recognizable at first except my knitting bag below my head, which had apparently served as a pillow. The last thing I remembered was being trapped inside the car unable to move, and then I must have fallen unconscious or something. A dull throbbing headache pounded away.

But here I was on the floor of what looked to be half of a small round building. Big Joe was huddled under a thin blanket beside me, snoring softly, while across the room, with his head propped up on his duffel bag, lay Max, arms crossed, looking surprisingly comfy despite the scratched face. There was a brass framed bed, now empty and tangled in bedclothes in the room's center, with a bright pink bra dangling from one of its nobs. Though the only window was shuttered tight, sunshine spilled through an open door to my left.

Slowly, I climbed to my feet, standing still until my legs were steady enough to carry me toward the scent of coffee. The round building had been divided in two by a curtain, with one half the bedroom, and the other a kitchen/living area.

Ahead of me with her back turned was the tallest woman I had ever seen, a shapely Amazon at least six foot four in pink shorts and a green hoodie, her cornrows tied back into a thick ponytail. She whipped around so fast I fell back a step. It took a moment for me to speak once I saw the machine gun she'd pulled out from somewhere.

"Is that necessary?" I asked.

"Sorry. Have to be supercharged 'round here," she said, lowering the gun. "You're Phoebe," she said with a big grin.

I sighed in relief. "I am, and you are?"

"Peaches."

Peaches. Of all the names I could think of for this magnificent armed and dangerous woman, Peaches wouldn't be it. "Glad to meet you, Peaches. Mind putting that thing away?"

"Surely." She tucked the rifle under a curtain beneath the sink.

"Is this your place?"

"Only for a bit. This be one of the watch posts, and me, I'm stationed here to wait for you. Now dat you come, I move on. Want coffee?"

"Yes, please," I said, stumbling forward to grasp the tin mug she offered.

"You sit," Peaches said, pointing to a ripped-out car seat propped against the wall. "Dat tree hit you guys on the head, smashed up Joe's truck something bad. Only down the road, so I saw you coming. I cut you out."

"So, you rescued us?" I asked, lowering myself into the seat and sipping the coffee. "Thanks." It was incredible, maybe the best coffee I'd ever tasted.

Peaches turned back to a woodstove and continued cooking something fragrant. "Yeah, I helped. Now I get to feed you and move you on to the next post before de gang gets here."

I swallowed hard. "Gang?"

"The Captain being chased by the Willies—mean bastards crack yer head open rather dan look at you. Other gangs want dem, too, but the Willies be the meanest and the worst. The leader is a piss-head."

"The Willies," I repeated. "The Captain is being chased by the Willies." It would be funny if it weren't so damn not. "Okay, so you were stationed to wait for us. Does that mean you work for the Captain?"

"Yeah." She turned around and strode toward me with something that smelled like heaven on a plate. "I work for the Captain for two years. I'm, like, one of his key helpers. He pays well and de other one not hard on de eyes, neither. Johnnycake. You eat up."

I took the johnnycake gratefully, and bit into something that tasted like a thick, yummy pancake, my mind whirling with questions. I swallowed quickly. "Does the Captain have red hair?"

Peaches grinned. "Yeah, he do. De Willies call him 'Captain Firebeard.'"

"That's my brother," I mumbled with my mouth full.

The large brown eyes widened. "Your brother? You kidding me?"

"I'm not kidding you," I said with a ridiculous swell of pride, "and I can't wait to see him, not to mention the one you say isn't hard on the eyes. That's Noel, my boyfriend." Was this, like, name-dropping?

She whistled between her teeth. "Well, shit. Yeah, dat explains everything—why we were told to treat you good, all de extra guards, all of it. If de Willies learn that you his sista, dey'd want you for ransom, all right. I get it now. You precious cargo. We be takin' care of you, girl. Now I wake up de others."

What followed from the adjoining room sounded like yelps of pain accompanied by a rush of patois between Peaches and Big Joe. In minutes, Peaches was back in the kitchen to continue stirring something in a frying pan. "You want fruit?" she said without turning. "Fruit hanging up outside."

Soon I was standing at the front door staring into the thick, steamy foliage as the sun beamed down through the jungle. The storm had downed trees, turned the road—if what I was staring at was a road—into a broken river of chunked-up pavement, mud, and tree trunks. It took a moment to tear away my gaze and realize that fruit dangled around the outside of the house like strings of edible beads—bananas, mangos, avocados, and a nubbly thing that looked like a hand grenade.

"Dat soursop," Peaches said, poking her head out. "Looks like shit, tastes like custard. I cut dat down for you." In seconds, she had whipped out a dagger, sliced the rope fastening the fruit, cut the palm-sized object in two, and scooped out a chunk of creamy fruit and seeds, handing me the morsel on the tip of her blade. Lord knows where that knife had been last, but I nibbled the fruit as offered while Peaches ducked back inside.

Whatever it was, it tasted exactly like sweet vanilla custard. Hand grenades that taste like pudding. I had, I decided, awoken in a tangled upside-down world where Toby and Noel were pirates who hired gangs to protect them against thugs called the Willies. If I didn't know better, I'd think I was on drugs.

I finished the sticky fruit, wiping my hands and the knife in water trapped in a banana leaf and stepped back into the kitchen. Peaches was yelling at Big Joe from the other room. In seconds she was shoving him into the kitchen while slapping him on the shoulder.

"Ah, Peaches, mi Peaches, you so mean to me," he cried, protecting his head from the assault.

"You shut up, you lug. Go to de truck and get de stuff before dey come."

Big Joe lumbered off, leaving me to stare at Peaches as she whacked a cell phone on the side of her smooth brown leg.

"De tower's down," she told me without looking up. "Happens all de time up here. Shit." She pulled out another phone and seemed happy with the signal.

In moments, she was speaking into the phone in perfectly modulated Colonial English. "Peaches, here. I must get a message to the Captain...Yes, that is correct. Tell him that the cargo has arrived in good condition. Our intention is to make the beach before nightfall, but we will be forced to take the long way around...Yes, that is the way it must be: the roads have been washed away. Wait for us there."

She disconnected and caught me staring. "Look, I speak Jamaican out of habit, see? But I was educated in England and have a PhD in engineering, which is absolutely useless to me, since nobody's hiring my ilk at the moment. Why don't you go into the bedroom and rouse that uncle of yours? We have to finish breakfast and get our asses out of here."

"Godfather," I corrected.

"What the hell?" We turned to see Max standing in the doorway, groggy, disheveled, and nearly as confused as I was. "Who the hell are you?" he asked, staring at our host.

I intervened. "Peaches, meet my godfather, Max. Max, Dr. Peaches here has a PhD in engineering but is currently protecting us against a gang of thugs called the Willies. She's going to take us to the coast to meet up with my brother, Captain Firebeard, and Noel, who..." I paused and turned to Peaches. "Does Noel have a nickname, too?"

"How about 'hottie'?" And she gave me a wicked grin.

We ate plates of something spicy and yellow while squeezed together on the car seat. Bundles and packs sat bound together in a heap ready for travel, including our plastic-wrapped luggage.

"I thought these were scrambled eggs," Max mumbled, shoveling down his food between gulps of coffee, "but they don't taste like any eggs I've ever eaten."

"Do you see a chook 'round here, mista?" Big Joe asked between mouthfuls. "Dis be ackee, de best."

Peaches, propped on a wooden crate, leaned over to swat Big Joe's bare leg. "You speak nice to these folks, Joe. This be de Captain's sister and de hottie's main squeeze."

"Main squeeze? You mean there are others?" I asked, looking up.

"Maybe dere is and maybe dere isn't," she said, wearing a sly little smile. She was probably only teasing, but most men I knew didn't abstain when away from their women for months at a time. It was something I tried not to think about. These days, not thinking about things had become a troubling habit.

"Are there any snakes in Jamaica?" I asked, changing the subject.

"Seven actually," Peaches said, back to the perfect English, "but

none that will kill you. We have other things that will kill you instead
—mostly big men with machine guns. The Willies are not the only
bunch of drug lords after the Captain and his booty."

The food stuck in my throat. "Drug lords?"

"Yeah, drug lords. They know that the Captain is sitting on some
magnificent loot and they aim to grab some of it. Besides, there is bad
blood between them."

I glanced over to Max, who had stopped eating to listen, too.
"Bad blood?"

"Yeah, goes back a year or two."

"Do they know what that loot is?" Max asked.

"Does not matter to them. If it can be sold, it will do the job. But
they know there is lots of treasure to be had, and the drug lords would
love to get their hands on some of that, especially Willie."

"Have you seen this treasure?" I asked, my mouth dry.

Peaches cleaned her plate with a piece of johnnycake. "We do not
talk about specifics."

Joe nodded. "De Captain is de pirate king—lots of de shiny
stuff."

"I said that we do not talk about it, Joe." Peaches cast him such a
ferocious look the big man actually cringed.

"Max, can I speak to you in private?" I said, jumping up.

"Sure. Let's step outside."

"Do not be going far now," Peaches called.

"Yeah, like we could," I remarked.

We linked arms and strolled out the door, hanging a right to follow
a tangled path that wove to the back of the building. Max shoved away
a curtain of vines and whistled. "Well, look at that: there's a river
down there."

An angry mass of muddy water churned its way through a gorge far
below. "Yeah, and it's not happy. So, Noel and Toby are holed up here
as pirate kingpins. Am I hearing right? And surely Jamaica isn't the
safest place for a hideaway?"

"Can't think of a better one right now, can you? The island's mostly
off Interpol's grid and has served as a hiding pace for hundreds
of years."

"Yeah, for real pirates, maybe, and that was before satellites and airplanes."

"Look, darlin', nowhere's safe these days, not for what those two are harboring. They must move around a lot, and this hideaway, wherever the hell it is we're going to, must be temporary. Don't fret, I'm sure they've got things all under control."

"Under control? Max, apparently there are hoards of armed drug lords hunting them down and we may be leading them right to them. Does that sound like being in control to you? We should never have come. What were we thinking? We should have ignored that postcard."

Max squeezed my shoulder. "But we didn't. We want to see them as much as they must want to see us. It's damn hard being separated from those you love for years at a time. Besides, Phoebe, this is the risk that Noel and Toby took when they came here. We have to have faith."

My comment died on my tongue when a shout echoed from the jungle away to our right. "Sounds like it's coming from down near the truck."

We dashed back to the kitchen where Peaches and Big Joe were already strapping on backpacks, Big Joe grasping each of my plastic-wrapped bags in his hand.

"Dey found mi chucky," Big Joe wailed, tucking a machete into his belt. "Dey gonna torch mi chucky!"

"Oh, shut up, Joe. Grab as much as you can carry," Peaches ordered us. "There's food and water in that sack and other stuff in the other. Pick up what you can and run!"

I shoved my tapestry bag into one backpack before shrugging it on as Peaches and Joe slung rifles over their shoulders and bolted out the door.

"Jesus. Semiautomatics?" Max muttered but there was no time for discussion as we scrambled after our hosts.

I had a faint hope that we'd find some four-wheel drive parked under a banana tree somewhere and just zoom off down the mountain road. Instead, we bounded through the undergrowth straight toward the edge of the cliff.

"I'm not liking where this is heading," I whispered as Big Joe hacked at a giant fern. Seconds later, Peaches and Joe were bush-whacking through the jungle where fallen trees covered with delicate orchids blocked our path. Something spicy laced the air as the sun penetrated the canopy in hot bright motes that illuminated plants with shiny red-leaf flowers. A bird with a long arced tail flitted through the greenery as hummingbirds and butterflies fluttered in jolts of color. I was temporarily mesmerized as we plunged through this paradise.

But that was squelched the moment we stood on the brink of the green abyss, me grasping some glossy-leaved plant and staring down into the impenetrable jungle. This was more like the side of a mountain than a cliff, I realized, feeling ridiculously relieved. Cliffs were bad, very bad, whereas mountains were...equally bad.

"So, where are the stairs?" I asked hopefully.

Men shouting behind us drowned out Peaches snicker. "Just move it!" she hissed.

"Move it where?" I said, staring down through the sharply angled incline. "Where's the path?"

She just jumped over the edge, reaching back long enough to grab my ankle and pull me down behind her. "Run!"

"Run how?" Running was not possible. Sliding, however, was.

So I ran, well, more like a long, painful headlong stumble interrupted by whamming into trees and getting tangled in vines and slapped in the face by twigs, over and over again. Blinded by greenery, I couldn't see where I was going. All I knew was that I was going down, and down some more, all of it at a furious pace. Though I could hear them crashing around me, I lost sight of Max and Big Joe, but Peaches stuck by me as much as possible, given our trajectory.

And it was a trajectory. There were moments when I was trip-running so fast I thought I'd never regain my footing, or even stop long enough to gulp for air. Once a vine snagged my ankle, pitching me upward, only to yank me back with a painful wallop until I landed on my stomach in the sodden foliage.

Peaches leaped back up beside me, sliced the vine, and got me back on my feet, where I struggled to shove air in my lungs even while still on the move. I wondered when, if ever, we'd reach the end. I tried different balancing maneuvers, galloping down muddy rain-slicked foliage while wearing a backpack being totally new for me. Staying upright no matter what seemed the only objective.

Meanwhile, men were shouting to one another behind us. A gun cracked the air. Afraid that Max had been shot, I gripped a vine and tried to halt my descent long enough to turn around. Peaches reached up and tugged me back into the path she was cutting ahead with her machete, leaving me with no choice but to keep stumbling after her down the mountainside.

And then we hit a gully of runoff sluicing through the jungle at the same moment that our descent abruptly sharpened. Clutching a frond, I calculated what to do as Peaches fell onto her butt and slid away out of sight. Shit and hell! I tried to leap the rivulet, which ended with me slipping in the mud and hurling down after her headfirst.

Turning myself around with a backpack was impossible. Now all my vulnerable bits were exposed to every little twig and rock. I thanked my leather jacket again and again while choking on the water streaming into my mouth. I kept trying to flip over until finally I latched on to a branch long enough to dig my feet into the mud and flip onto my butt to continue my downward slide.

We broke through the jungle into a banana plantation, though it took a few seconds to realize that those blue plastic bags in those bent-over trees whizzing by were actually bananas. I could see Peaches zooming in the gully far ahead and Big Joe and Max still on their feet plowing away to the left.

More gunshots cracked the air behind us.

Panicking, I turned to catch sight of men breaking through the trees—five or six of them hurtling toward us. By the time I was facing front again, it was just in time to witness me ramming into Peaches.

The impact hurled both of us off the edge of bank straight into the churning waters of the Rio Grande, though I didn't know the name of the river at the time. I was too busy keeping my head above water.

My feet scraped the bottom but the current was sweeping me downstream in a kind of running swim. My sole objective became how to get that backpack off before the depth dropped. Backpack, jacket, sneakers—all had become a liability.

Peaches bobbed beside me. "Keep going!" she cried. "Let the river take you! Our boat's gone!"

What boat? I didn't know anything about a boat. Coughing up water, I struggled to unfasten the backpack without losing grip of it. I needed that thing, but I also needed to survive. Peaches had already ditched hers but I couldn't see what she'd done with it, if anything. She was trying to stay with me but her attempts were foiled again and again as the river bounced us along, whipping her further and further away. Somehow I ended up close to shore while she bounced along in the swirling center.

That river—a muddy, raging, bucking creature with its own evil intent—was pulling us apart, sending her hurling ahead as I struggled to stay afloat. My feet lost their traction as I tried to steer closer to shore.

Flotsam and debris whammed into me as I lost my footing. I was a strong swimmer but the jacket, the pack—everything—was just too damn heavy. And then I hit a tree snagged crosswise among some rocks and managed to cling there long enough to shrug off the back-pack. I had some foolish notion that I could hang on to the pack somehow, a hope that ended when the current wrenched the thing from my grip. I watched the pack become a black speck bobbing downstream before I draped myself over the tree and started peeling off my jacket and sneakers.

I figured I just needed to free myself from the soaked clothes to reach the shore. If I could only climb over the rocks, maybe push against the current, I might reach safety. But a glance behind me nixed that theory, too: a boatload of armed men were paddling toward me—six men, one riding the prow with a machine gun slung over his shoulder.

Blinking like crazy, I double-checked: yes, they were definitely paddling a flat-bottom boat in my direction, though the river heaved them forward without much effort required. I tried pushing myself away from the tree but one arm was tangled in my jacket's sleeve, which had snagged among the branches. There I hung, kicking and squirming as the boat rolled toward me.

In moments, the boat thudded into the tree while the men yipped and hooted. By then my jacket was nothing but a sodden thing bunched around one arm like a boa constrictor while my sweater had ridden up over my shoulders. One big guy plucked me up by the sweater's collar while another sliced the jacket sleeve in two. In seconds they had tossed me facedown into the bottom of the boat like a line-caught tuna, where I remained shivering as the boat rocked off down the river.

I was soaked, exhausted, and terrified. All I could see from that angle were a bunch of bare toes in sandals, gun cases, knife holsters, and packs of ammunition amid chocolate wrappers and empty beer cans rattling around the aluminum boat. The rocking was churning my gut, though I suspected the breakfast had something to do with it. I decided that the safest thing for me to do was keep quiet, not like I had energy for much else.

No one spoke to me directly, anyway, though they continued shouting overhead in patois so thick I couldn't grasp much more than the occasional word. One of them rested his foot on my bare back like I was some kind of trophy catch, while another plucked my bra strap followed by a derisory hoot.

Shit, shit, shit. I'd been captured by a drug gang, which had to make me as good as dead. I figured that this was all about waiting to reach dry ground before they either had their fun or finished me off— probably both, in that order. I could see no way out. The one time I tried to struggle onto my hands and knees, that foot pressed me down with such force my chin banged against the bottom.

Maybe it took minutes, maybe hours, but eventually the boat ground up against the shore. My captors leaped out, one of them hoisting me up and over his shoulders like a duffel bag. With my head dangling down within inches of his grimy shorts, I watched the churning water below change to shale and then to jungle path. The stench of wet body combined with jostling gait was like a call to action for my gut.

"Stop!" I cried. "I'm going to—" But then it hit, the lovely projec- tile vomit that spewed torrents of half-digested ackee all over the man's butt. He dropped me like a sack of potatoes and jumped away screaming as if I'd just ruined his thousand-dollar suit. I toppled onto the jungle floor in a heap.

By then all I could do was bend over retching. I was vaguely aware of the men shouting around me and managed to lift my gaze long enough to see my carrier guy scraping his butt off against a tree while the others laughed. Then somebody hoisted me to my feet.

"You stand?" he asked. I turned to look at a skinny little guy with a concerned expression, opened my mouth to speak, and then promptly blacked out.

❧ 12 ❧

I awoke in a darkened room, totally naked. Flinging away the sheet, I stood trembling, trying to think. Had I been raped? Hell, surely I'd remember that much. Running a mental body check, I realized that I was scratched and bruised, but not violated. Otherwise, I was sticky with sweat and unsteady on my feet. Either the world was on fire or I was, because everything seemed burning hot—my forehead, my chest. Trying to think further was useless.

I stumbled back to the edge of the bed, certain I was alone. After the river and the vomiting, I remembered nothing, but evidently my captors carried me here—wherever here was—stripped me, and put me to bed. *Shit.* My gut lurched at the thought of being naked and helpless surrounded by a bunch of mean, drug-addled men. And I could not stop shivering despite that sense of internal combustion.

Gradually, my eyes acclimatized. Slivers of light from a shuttered window cast enough illumination for me to recognize what looked to be an ordinary bedroom. There was even a bedside lamp, which I flicked on. Well, damn, it was true: I had been tucked under a flowered sheet in a concrete-walled room, empty but for a bureau. Though barely furnished, the place could have belonged to any suburban home if it weren't for the pounding of the sea and what I took to be the steady far-off drone of a helicopter.

Wrapping the sheet around myself, I padded over to the window. Not a window, I realized, but a door with horizontal slats that levered open directly to the night air. I inhaled the sea breeze as I brought my eyes up to the slats. A three-quarter moon hovered above a balcony overlooking the ocean. And the pounding of those waves could have been the beating of my own heart and that supposed helicopter noise was a generator, I realized.

Visions of escape fired me. I sought a handle, a lock, a something, but the wooded shutter had been bolted into the concrete frame and no amount of rattling could loosen the thing. Even the handle had been knocked off.

Panicking, I circled the room, finding four other shuttered windows equally secured, plus one bathroom, and one interior door, bolted shut. Pressing my ear against the wood, I heard men's voices coming from somewhere deep inside the house—the Willies. I was imprisoned by a bunch of drug lords, and if I didn't escape, who knew what they'd do to me?

I checked every drawer of the bureau for tools or something I could use as a weapon—all empty—and even sought out a closet, which didn't exist. The room was totally barren, and though the oddest prison I could imagine, a prison nonetheless.

Finally, I entered the tiny bathroom, flicked on the light, and studied the toilet and the sink, each of which were spotless and seemingly brand new. A cake of soap, a bottle of shampoo, and a towel had been neatly laid out on the counter. I stared in the mirror at my pale mud-streaked face with the shaggy red hair leaping in Medusa-like curls around my head. Splashing water over myself did little to improve the effect, but at least cooled me down.

Being a prisoner was one thing, being a naked prisoner stripped of all my belongings was something else again. First dress, then make an exit plan, in that order. I ripped up the sheet to make a basic toga, sitting down periodically do regain my strength before resuming the effort. I had just finished tying the ends around my neck when the door flung open behind me.

"Holy shit! What have you done with my sheet, woman?"

I stared at a small, wiry middle-aged lady in a bright red velvet dressing gown standing hands on hips. Behind her, a man in a tracksuit held a tray and a machine gun.

"Do you expect me to lay around naked?" I asked, backing away.

The woman approached, brandishing a fist. "I should whup your ass! You come to my house and rip up my sheets? That's how your mother brought you up?"

"Nobody's going to whoop me without a fight!" I cried. "And why are you talking to like I'm your guest? I'm a prisoner! Etiquette doesn't count. I tore up your precious sheets because I'm naked!"

By now I had scrambled onto the bed and stood plotting an escape. Maybe I could tackle her in hand-to-hand combat, maybe even surprise-attack her gunslinger pal, too, but the chances of me escaping the house without being shot were slim. Besides, I wasn't up to the effort: I was sweating heavily and my legs were quaking.

"I took off your clothes because you were soaked and practically as bare as the day you was born. Now get down off that bed and eat your supper!" she yelled, pointing at the tray.

I just gaped. "So, you're, like, my mommy now?"

She shook her head. "Your mommy? The hell—like I'd have a fool girl like you as my daughter. I don't want you here any more than you want to be here, but my Willies brought you, so here you stay! Now, you either eat and stay alive, or I'll be coming back to shove that cooking down your scrawny little throat. We need you in good shape."

"Why? What are you planning to do with me? Look, all I want is get out of here and find my friends, okay?" That was me trying to sound reasonable but coming off whiny. "Did your Willies capture them, too?"

"You crazy? Think I'm going to tell you anything, girl? You'll stay here until we say otherwise. And you do one more thing to damage my stuff and I will come back here and whup you personally, no matter what." With that, she stomped out, muttering as the dude slammed the door shut. The bolt shot closed.

"Wait!" I said, stumbling to the door. "I want to speak to the boss! Let me out of here!" I pounded the door with my fists in one of those

utterly pointless actions I'd seen in the movies. Then I caught myself.
Better to save my energy for something useful. Hell knows I had little
enough to spare.

If only I had a few sturdy tools—something for pounding, or
prying, or levering—maybe I'd get somewhere, but the room was
empty, empty, empty, and my whole body was trembling to the point
where I thought I'd pass out.

Maybe food would help. Shivering, I checked the tray and found a
plate of something curried on rice, a bottle of water, and a can of Red
Stripe beer. The last thing I wanted to do was eat but I needed energy
so I picked at the spicy mix, finding it hot enough to require liberal
dousing of both the beer and the water. In the end I swilled more than
I ate before falling back on the bed, dizzy and queasier than ever.
Maybe it was the beer, or the carb-laced food, or I'd picked up a bug,
but within minutes, I'd passed out again.

I awoke with the sound of men's voices outside. Bolting off the
bed, I was shocked to find that it was now daylight but the world
seemed even more feverish with heat and humidity. I couldn't tell
whether the world was spinning or I was. Men's voices seemed to be
traveling through the house; their footsteps and hoots reverberated
through the walls. It felt like each step was squashing me alive.

Stumbling back to the bed, I hunched over my knees trying to
quell the nausea. I sat there for a minute, shivering, until I noticed a
pile of clothes on the floor. It took every scrap of energy I had left to
pull on that silky white nightie, the panties and bra, before flopping
back on the bed where I blacked out again.

I don't know how long I stayed under this time but a nasty tangle
of vivid dreams tied my emotions in knots. Visions of leering men and
muddy rivers dragging me down. I was soaked, always soaked. I vaguely
remember someone making me drink water—or maybe I was
drowning—and something cool pressed to my forehead. "Noel?" I
whispered. Someone laughed and I blacked out again.

From then on, I just slept. Hours later, I sat up, restored, though
still weak, but able to make my way to the toilet.

When I returned to the room, my hostess was sitting primly on the
edge of the bed wearing a red silk gown and holding a glass of some

gray filmy liquid on a silver tray. It was a sight so bizarre I thought it must be the fever.

She got to her feet the moment she saw me and held out the glass. "You drink this up. Make you feel better."

I stared from the gray liquid to her made-up face, noting how her lipstick matched the coral hue of her dress. She could be fifty years old or a hundred. "What is it?" I asked.

"Noni juice," she said. "Grows near the beach and tastes like shit, but best thing for what ails you. Cures everything. Drink."

"It looks like poison," I said, taking the glass, stifling the flash thought that maybe I could grab the tray and whack her with it. Stupid.

"Tastes like it, too, but if I wanted to kill you, I'd have done it by now, and it wouldn't be slow-style, I can tell you. If I had a choice, I'd just shoot you in the head and be done. Need you alive, he said. Now drink. Don't taste, just swallow," she warned.

"What's your name?" I asked, taking a sip. Oh, yuck. She was right about the taste.

"We're not going to be friends anytime soon, girl, but you can call me Lady Willie."

"Lady Willie?"

"Drink!"

So I gulped it back, trying not to taste the foul stuff as it slithered its way down. I shuddered, nearly dropping the glass. "Blech!" My gut lurched but somehow held its contents.

"Pretty much sums it up. Now, you follow me. It's time. They're back now and he's ready to see you." She turned, taking the tray with her, and opened the door where two armed guys leaned against the wall.

I placed the glass on the bureau. "Who's back?"

"My Willie."

"You mean, the main Willie, Mr. Willie?"

"Just move it," she ordered, "Or I'll get my boys to drag you."

I hurried after her, bracing myself against the walls as she dashed down a set of stairs and through rooms flooded in sunshine. Squinting,

I made out big modern sectional couches and tables that could have come from any high-end store.

Bright paintings of tropical scenes splashed color above replicas of ancient art, which seemed to take up every spare inch. A mix of wide-screen televisions and computers occupied some rooms, while a confusing combo of ancient and modern art others. I was temporarily transfixed by what looked to be a replica of an ancient Roman bust wearing earphones sitting on top of a stack of magazines, when one of the Willies shoved me hard.

"Watch it! I'm coming." I snapped. The guy just grinned.

Room after room and pile after pile of stuff passed until finally we stopped. Lady Willie knocked on the door at the end of a corridor, which was promptly opened by a beautiful, skimpily dressed young woman.

"Hi, Gloria." She smiled. "You brought her?"

"Yeah, Crystal, I brought her. Now move your ass outta there and let her pass. The boys are waiting for you downstairs."

Crystal shrugged and sashayed away, smiling over her shoulder and finger-fluttering a little wave at Lady Willie.

Gloria nodded to one of the men who half dragged me into the room.

"Boss?" he called. "She's here." He flung me into a chair and left.

❧ 13 ❧

All I saw were the floor-to-ceiling windows looking out onto a long balcony. Blue sea, sunshine, postcard views—was I in some holiday resort for the dammed?

But there had to be an exit there somewhere, too.

I was on my feet in seconds and soon found a sliding door not more than three yards away, but even after I applied the full force of my shoulder, the slider didn't budge. Locked? Wedged? I tried again and again, not thinking clearly, only focusing on escape. It was as if the blue waves beckoned to me in the cove beyond. God, how I wanted to be free—in that water, anywhere but here.

Wait, I needed something to smash the glass. I scanned the room, my gaze flashing through a cluttered den with plenty of objects scattered around, the specifics of which I ignored until my attention landed on a gilded figurine perched on the desk nearby. Heavy —perfect.

Picking it up, I swung back toward the windows, ready to hurl the Aztec replica in a two-armed sling, when suddenly, seemingly out of nowhere, someone grabbed one arm, twisted it hard, and forced me to release the statue. Clutching me by the scruff of the neck, he then rammed my head into the glass, and the world cracked into pain.

"Stop it!" I cried out, clawing at the hands that held me.

"This is not how you are to behave, Miss Phoebe. Very bad girl are you," a deep voice said overhead. "Victor!" he boomed.

"Yes, Boss?"

"Miss Phoebe does not know it is not polite to touch other people's things. She now wants to take a look outside. Why don't you show her the sights?"

"Yes, Boss."

I was too dizzy to realize what was happening, so when the grip released me and I fell to my knees, all I could do was stare at the tiles as they tipped and shifted. And then, just as quickly, I was yanked back on my feet, in a daze, as a big hand flicked up a lock on the sliders, and I was shoved outside.

"You wish to see the sights, Miss Phoebe?" Another voice was saying as he steered me straight for the balcony railing. "I show you."

I tried to speak but being crushed against the marble railing and held halfway over the edge squelched that. I thought for sure he planned to throw me over. For terrifying seconds, I was made to stare down at the surf crashing on the rocks, a dizzying, seething boil of sea, which would ordinarily thrill me but was having the opposite effect now. In fact, I had the urge to vomit.

I kicked out, trying to lever myself back to solid ground but the man held me with one hand on my nightdress, the other gripping the waistband of my undies. Since that waistband was elastic, I could easily slip out of the panties like a sausage from its casing and hurl into the sea. I blinked, staring down to where I might plunge straight onto the rocks below. Just a few yards further down, it looked a smooth patch of deep blue swirling around a rocky outcrop—as if I had a choice of landing spots.

"This, Miss Phoebe," the deep bass voice said nearby, "is where you thought you could run. Not a good idea, I'd say. We are surrounded by jungle and sea with no place to go. Victor, illustrate my point."

Victor hauled me back, using my arm as steerage as he directed me down the long veranda. We passed hurricane-strewn deck chairs, upended flower pots, and grazed tables plastered by leaves and fronds, all whizzing by as I stumbled down the end of the deck. I then was half flung over another railing and forced to stare over at jungle this time. Glimpses of a brackish cove with something metal glinting amid the mangroves was in my sights but I also noted how the balcony seemed to extend all around the house.

"So you see, Miss Phoebe, you are prisoner on my island fortress," the boss voice said. "You will not be going anywhere until your purpose has been served. Now I will explain that purpose. Return her to the study, Victor."

Victor wrenched me away from the railing and swung me back the way we'd come. Ahead, a bald man dressed in a white linen suit sauntered along but I was still too dizzy to pick up much detail. Once he stepped into the den and I was thrown back into the chair, all I could do was wrestle the world back into focus by shoving my head between my knees waiting for the spinning to stop. I touched the swelling lump on my temple and struggled not to retch.

"I understand that you are not in the best of health," the boss voice remarked.

"Think having my head slammed against the glass helps?" I lifted my gaze then, trying to make out his features, but with the sun shining straight into my eyes and the bastard standing with his back to the light, that was useless. All I could do was put my head back into my hands and will the world to stop spinning.

"Call for tea!" the boss voice boomed. There was a scurry of movement. A door slammed somewhere. Voices followed.

Minutes passed with me barely moving. The last thing I needed was another bout of projectile vomiting—not that this guy didn't deserve to have his suit splattered. I kept thinking of Toby and Noel and Max, worry and fear churning with my longing.

Finally a glass of tea appeared before my face. I took the mug and sipped, tasting sweet ginger and apple combined—simple, and soothing. Several gulps later, the world began leveling and my stomach began to subside. I risked leaning back in the chair and took a deep breath.

"That is better," the boss said from somewhere behind me. "I trust that you are now able to listen and speak." It wasn't a question.

"Are you the head Willie?" I asked.

"I am Roger Williams, yes. My people have a great sense of humor

and find calling my organization 'the Willies' to be amusing. Ha, ha—
they so enjoy their little jokes. But never mind: if they treat me with
the respect I deserve, they can call my organization whatever they
please. The results are the same. A nation of comedians, we are."

"Yeah, you guys crack me up."

He chuckled to himself. "Yes, well, until we are on more friendly
terms, you must call me Mr. Williams."

"What do you want with me, Mr. Williams?" I turned as he took
the chair opposite mine and got a good look at him at last.

What did I expect—a sweatsuited dude with gold chains and a
sideways baseball hat? Roger Williams was not my idea of a drug lord,
not with that plummy island accent elevated by doses of post-
secondary education. Did they send drug lords to university
these days?

In his early thirties and of trim middle height, he wore a suit of
which Rupert Fox would have approved—definitely expensive and
perfectly tailored—only Foxy would never wear his shoes without
socks, nor a black T-shirt under white linen, nor a big chunk of
diamond drilled into one ear. And never, ever that shiny shaved head—
definitely not the shaved head.

I studied him in silence while he watched me back. "I see I surprise
you," he said as he sipped a can of soda through a straw.

"I thought you'd be older," I said.

He grinned, a big beautiful smile that on any other person would
cause me to smile back. "Now, why would you think that?"

"Because of your wife," I said.

"I do not have a wife, Miss Phoebe."

"But Lady Will—I mean Gloria, the woman who sort of nursed me
when I was sick..."

And then he slapped his thigh and laughed, a big boom that filled
the room. "That is my *Auntie* Gloria!" He laughed as if that was the
funniest thing he'd ever heard. Suddenly sobering, he added: "Auntie
Gloria is all I have left of my family."

"Oh," I said.

He slammed the can on a side table, his eyes locked on mine.
"Family is the most important part of life, do you agree? We all need

unconditional love and loyalty. That is why you have come to my lovely island, Miss Phoebe. You wish to be reunited with those you love—your brother and maybe a certain handsome archaeologist?"

I straightened. Now we were getting down to it. "What are you talking about?"

"Do not play games with me, Miss Phoebe." He wagged his finger. "I know all about your liaisons, all about your brother, Tobias, and his little band of thieves, and your godfather, too."

Max must have gotten away. If he hadn't, I'm sure he'd be sitting right here with me now. Still, best not to mention him. "You're a fine one to talk about thieves," I said. "Look at you, terrorizing this island you call home. Your reputation precedes you." I'd never heard of him before this, of course, but I recognize an inflated ego when I saw one.

"And you are trying to change the subject. Very well, we will leave that topic for a moment while I endeavor to improve your education."

"How do you propose to do that?"

He grinned. "By teaching you a few timely lessons. Pay attention now. Here is the first lesson. Whatever it is that you heard about me, the fact is that I only discipline those who fail to respect me, while those that do as I say are amply rewarded. Mind that point carefully, Miss Phoebe, since it involves you." He leaned back, crossed his legs, and appeared genuinely amused. "No one suffers unless they bring it upon themselves. You may call that terrorizing but I call it justice."

I almost choked. "Are you kidding me? Are you suggesting that you are some kind of benevolent drug-dealing dictator?"

He studied his can of Ting. "'Drug-dealing dictator'—nice alliteration. I like that. Not a dictator, no, but I would do a very good job of ruling this country, given the opportunity. Instead, I rule the underground economy, perhaps the most important force of any nation."

"A criminal by any other name."

"Careful not to throw stones, Miss Phoebe," he said, looking up. "Crime is afoot in your family, too. Back to my point: I employ many people, and keep trade going all over Jamaica. The Willies are a valued part of the underground economy in what is really a very poor country, at best. That is your first lesson. Do you understand me so far?"

"Sure. You want me to believe that the drugs you smuggle into the islands benefit Jamaica, when I know that the only ones who win are the rich cats at the top of the heap, cats like you."

"Tsk-tsk." He shook his finger at me. "A poor student, I see. And very disrespectful, too. This disappoints me, but let us go on to lesson number two so that you may improve. You come from the great white north with your tiny white mind. You think you know how the less fortunate live because you hold liberal views. In truth, you only see what is before your eyes but fail to understand what lies beneath. To you, my people are just the poor black folk who you tip to pour your drinks and make your beds in your fancy hotels. Perhaps you express kindness to my people in terms of those tips but your condescension reeks. You do not, and never will, understand our lives."

"That's true up to a point. I mean, of course no one can understand how another person lives, but I am aware of the skewed power and circumstances between rich and poor, black and white. It sickens me, but it's how society has evolved and now we have to try and fix it fast. But you'll never convince me that the drug trade somehow makes life better for your people."

"While my people bow and scrape to the rich tourists coming to our paradise, every cent of real profit goes to the big conglomerates. All these resorts are owned by foreigners. Nobody takes care of islanders but we islanders. My people starve while craving all the nice things they see the tourists waving before their eyes, or on television, so it is I, Mr. Williams—" he pointed to his chest "—who gives them what they want. Indeed I do. Do not look so skeptical, Miss Phoebe. Open your mind. I also run many a children's charity across Jamaica, make no mistake about it."

"Oh, sure you do—at a price." I didn't know where this was going but I knew I wouldn't like it.

He lifted his hands. "There is a price for everything, Miss Phoebe. That is the first lesson everyone learns on this earth. How could you miss something so fundamental? For every thing you say to me, there will be a consequence."

Didn't I know it, yet somehow I couldn't stop myself. "I just bet. You said so yourself: if your workers step out of line, they pay. Where's the benefit to your people there? That makes you nothing more than a power-wielding dictator."

He bared his teeth. That was no smile. "My men work hard, yes, and in exchange I feed their children, and buy them cars and nice homes. The women service my men and in exchange they receive nice clothes and pretty baubles—all fair trade. Right now, under this very roof, I am rewarding my men for a job well done. I offer many perks. I am an excellent employer and give generously to the needy. Is that not true, Victor?"

"Yes, Boss," said a voice somewhere behind me. I lacked the energy to look.

"Let me guess: if Victor doesn't agree, he gets both knees broken or shot at dawn? Like you said—consequences."

Head Willie only chuckled, shaking his head the whole time, but beneath the urbane exterior, I sensed a viper ready to spring. "I see you do not learn your lessons well."

But Phoebe McCabe always gets in the last word. Even if it's her last. I leaned forward. "What you've just described sounds like monetized slavery. You can't honestly believe I'm going to buy that, do you? Sure, you bring money into the country, and with it comes drugs, guns, and violence—the same as the drug trade everywhere. Who are you trying to kid, Mr. Willie? You're just a piece of scum."

Okay, so I wasn't gunning for Miss Congeniality, either.

He lunged. My eyes locked on his as his fingers encircled my throat and pressed. Spots flared in my eyes. "You speak with so much disrespect, Miss Phoebe. You do not learn your lessons well."

I was hardly in the position to comment, so I gurgled while waiting for those fingers to squeeze the life out of me. But they didn't, they just pressed for a few moments before releasing me. I fell back against the chair.

"You cause me to lose my temper," he said as he stood above me flexing his fingers. "But I am a patient man. You will learn how to treat me. Roger Williams will not be disrespected."

"When did...*disrespect* become...a verb?" I rasped.

He frowned. "I wondered the same thing. Never mind, you will still *respect* me."

"Why?" I croaked.

"Because you wish to stay alive." He smiled, his body relaxing again. "I consider that a very good reason, grammatical issues aside."

"What do you...want?" I asked. I knew, of course: I was to be either ransom or bait, maybe both.

He moved his head from side to side like he was the one who just had his neck squeezed. "I want to get back what is mine, Miss Phoebe, and receive just compensation for all that I have suffered."

"What...have you suffered?" I asked, rubbing my throat.

"The loss of my family. Your brother has cost me the most important part of my existence—my father, my mother, and my sister—and for this he will pay and you also. You will be my revenge."

I laughed, or tried to, but my cough wasn't fooling anybody. "Me? How can I be your...revenge? Do you think you're going to...ransom me?"

He cast me a lethal grin. "That will come naturally, but first I will carve you up in little pieces right before your brother's eyes."

14

A head-jerk from Willie signaled Victor to yank me to my feet. "Just ask me to stand and I'll stand!" I cried, like that made a difference. In seconds, I was shoved across the den into an adjoining room and slammed into a wheeled chair before a big computer. Two guys were fiddling with the controls behind the flickering screen.

"What the hell is going on?" I asked, still talking like I had some say in the matter.

"What is going on, Miss Phoebe, is that you are about to see your brother and your lover on Skype," Head Willie said with a feral grin. "Does this excite you?"

Any flutter of anticipation I experienced was poisoned with dread. Would seeing me like this provoke Toby and Noel to do something foolish? There was the matter of the Raphael, which I believed to be at the heart of my kidnapping, no matter what Willie said. But was my life worth a masterpiece of historic and artistic importance?

I'd pondered that question multiple times and from every possible angle, and my answer always came out the same: no. A single life should never be traded for art of such significance. Of course, it's not easy to hold on to that position when that life happens to be your own. It might even be harder when the choice involves someone you love.

"Why can't my team get the equipment working?" Boss Man was saying. "What is the holdup? I have provided ample time to correct this situation and I am running out of patience. Why is there no screen? I need a signal now!"

"The hurricane, Boss," a little man squealed as he fiddled away. "All de cell towers be down. Be trying for de cell signal."

"Try harder. I pay you to solve problems, not whine about them. What about a satellite link?" Head Willie boomed. "Do I have only idiots working for me?"

"No, Boss, but I can't get de fix," a guy in a striped T-shirt said.

"Careful, boys," I said. "Your benevolent leader just might break a limb if you don't comply."

"I'd rather break yours first," Willie said, leaning over me, "so I suggest you be quiet, Miss Phoebe, and conserve your strength. You will need it before this day is over."

That ominous declaration shut me up. I subsided inside myself while nursing my bruised throat and throbbing temple, wondering how the hell I was going to get out of this one. For once, I had no former MI6 agent in the wings and my own resources seemed pitifully inadequate—no phone, no energy, no Peaches, no Max—nothing and no one. And now I was going to be used to harm the people I loved?

"Victor, return Miss Phoebe to her room. There she shall stay until these idiots get the system working."

I leaped to my feet before the henchman could wrench another limb from its socket, but that didn't stop him from shoving me. I banged my knee on the rolling chair as he pushed me through the study and up a different set of stairs. As we traveled down a long corridor, we passed a half-opened door where I glimpsed men sprawled over chairs watching something out of my view. A powerful reek of pot emanated from within. I tried to get my bearings, memorizing the lay of the land, but then Victor took yet another set of stairs thus throwing me off.

Soon he was pushing me into my prison and onto the bed. I lay back in silence watching the hunger flicker in his eyes. I realized I must be quite a sight in the almost transparent silk nightie wearing nothing but my bra and panties beneath.

He was a big man, selected no doubt because of his imposing size and bulging muscles, and the glint in his eyes told me that inflicting pain was as much a passion as a career choice. He'd love nothing more than to let himself loose on me right then.

While he struggled with his urges, I plotted my defense strategy, futile though it might be. I'd kick him. I was good at kicking and maybe I'd even live long enough to escape the room.

Suddenly, he reined himself in and retreated quickly, bolting the door behind him. I stared at the ceiling, breathing deeply, trying to steady my heart.

Oh, hell. I was in such deep trouble. I needed a plan before Willie let these hounds loose on me, which I figured he would soon enough. But I was short of ideas. Without a phone, I couldn't alert anyone to my whereabouts, not that they could easily reach me, anyway. And the place was crawling with big gun-toting, probably trigger-happy men, and Willie must have done everything possible to protect his bastion in other ways. If Noel and Toby did try to storm the estate, there'd be a bloodbath, which I did not want on my hands, at any cost.

Besides, Noel and Toby were not violent men. Well, actually, Noel had his moments but never without just cause. In any case, I couldn't picture even him launching some kind of SWAT team to rescue me. Where would he wrestle up those kinds of resources?

So, all the people who had ever helped me when I needed it—the ones who actually cared—may as well be on another planet, including Rupert and Evan, who I'd dispatched to Tahiti.

And I'd left my Foxy phone behind and turned my other one off, which was probably at the bottom of the river by now along with my poor yarn. I didn't even know if Max was all right or if Peaches and Big Joe had reached safety. What if something had happened to them? Alone in this fortress of ruthlessness, I was screwed.

After a few minutes, I dragged myself into the bathroom and tended to my throat and temple. A blue-black lump had formed on my brow, a bruise that only added to the growing assortment covering my body, and my throat now took on a similar cast. I looked pathetic, I *was* pathetic. Why did I always end up in these situations? Because I chased rather than led? Because I was always reacting instead acting on my own moral code? Did I even have a moral code? I used to think so but now I wasn't so sure.

Crud. I could do with some ice, a cold drink, a sandwich, maybe, definitely a hug. I sat down on the edge of the toilet and cried.

By the time Gloria entered the room with a tray later, I was all wrung out from searching yet again for an escape hatch while mewing away like a wounded cat. I sat on the bed, staring at the wall, my fingers aching to knit.

She slid the tray on the bureau. Behind her stood another armed dude with features frozen into a look of cool distain—part of the House of Willie uniform.

"What did my brother do to your family?" I asked.

"Are you speaking to me?" the woman demanded, turning with hands on hips.

"Yes. I asked what my brother did to your family. Willie said that you were his aunt, and that he'd lost his mother, father, and sister. They must be your relatives, too."

"So? My brother is dead to me now. My Willie's the only one who ever saw me straight."

"What happened?"

"What, you think I'm going to sit down and have a cozy chat with you? Not happening, girlie."

"Do you have children?" I was just looking for signs of humanity.

"What's that got to do with you?"

"Just asking. Look at me." I pointed to my head. "I've been slammed against the wall, half thrown over the balcony, and threatened to within an inch of my life, yet I still don't know why. I haven't done anything to you or your nephew. Is it too much to ask for a little explanation?"

She stepped toward me, the rosy satin of her dress shimmering in the lamplight and what looked to be a huge pink diamond ring sparkling on her middle finger. With her lips drawn into a permanent frown, nothing in her expression registered sympathy. "You probably got what you deserved." Standing over me, she stared at my temple for a minute. "You do something to get him riled?"

I saw no point in lying. "Okay, so I tried to escape by smashing the glass with one of his figurines."

That almost provoked a smile but this one kept herself well under wraps. "So you got him mad?"

"Yes, and I don't care. Do you think I'm going to sit there and let some muscle guy push me around?"

She assessed me for a moment. "You have spirit, I'll say that much for you, but you must be pretty dim. You're in a house filled with armed men so you start picking things up and start throwing them? You touch one of his precious oldies and that'll make Willie go as crazy as a stuck pig."

"Oldies? Do you mean all this stuff I see around here is real?"

"Surely. My Willie collects them, not that I can see much point in it, but that's me."

Willie was a collector? Where'd he get that stuff—the Roman busts, the Aztec statues? But I didn't have time to ponder that, not now that I had her talking. "But what's this about my brother supposedly stealing his family—your family? My brother's no kidnapper, and I don't mean because he's in a wheelchair. That may be your nephew's thing but not his."

She cocked her head and stared down at me. "You fishing, girl? Think I'm going to fall for the sympathy routine because your brother's a cripple? Your brother gets no sympathy around here, not with what he's sitting on."

"Whatever he's 'sitting on' isn't for his own benefit. He's preserving posterity by keeping certain items out of the hands of private collectors and greedy drug-running thugs."

And she guffawed. "You're a dim-witted fool if you believe that."

"It's true," I protested, my indignation real. "He's not in this for himself."

She shook her head. "Everybody's in it for himself, and don't you forget it, girlie. Now eat up."

"Wait!" I said, climbing to my feet. "Tell me how my family is involved with your family—just that much, please."

"Not happening. I said that you'll find out whatever my Willie wants you to know when he wants you to know it. Now eat because it's gonna be a long night."

"Why is it going to be a long night?"

But Gloria was already at the door.

"Wait!" I cried, stumbling after her. "How did my brother hurt your brother?"

But the door slammed in my face.

I MUST HAVE DOZED BECAUSE THE NEXT THING I KNEW, VICTOR WAS kicking my leg. I jolted up and almost returned the insult on reflex but stopped myself. Instead, I allowed him to push and shove me all the way downstairs and back toward the computer room while feigning dizziness along the way. Actually, I didn't feel half-bad physically by then but there was no way I'd let him see that.

This time we took his second route and when we passed the room I'd noted earlier, I fell to my knees in a pseudo-faint. As I lay doubled over, I got a good look inside: lots of men lounging around smoking and drinking while a handful of women stripteased to a drum-pounding rhythm. The reek of marijuana was so thick inhaling would probably send me to la-la land.

Rifles sat propped up against the walls but none of those dudes looked in the mood to use them. A breeze cleared the haze long enough for me to realize that a glass door had been opened to the night breeze.

My yelp as Victor wrenched me to my feet didn't provoke so much as a glance from the men. Drugs, booze, sex—the boys must be reaping in their good-behavior awards.

Vince half dragged me the rest of the way while I took in details through half-closed lids. The house was alive with lights and noise compared to earlier. A few men leaned against the doorjambs drinking beer and laughing with half-dressed women hanging on—working girls, I figured.

"Hey dere, Vic. You get dat girl for de night?" one guy asked, leering at me.

"Not yet," my guard called back. "But when I do, she'll be a'crying for mi big stick." He pumped his hips in case buddy missed the point.

The man howled with laughter while my brain struggled with the implication. *Was I going to be Victor's reward? Oh, Lord, no.*

Lady Gloria waved as I stumbled through the den. "You be good now, girlie," she called out. In seconds, I was slammed back in the rolling chair before the computer screen with Willie and his two tech guys standing by.

"We are ready at last, Miss Phoebe." He indicated the screen, which was now flipping through postcard shots of what I presumed to be Jamaica.

My response was to close my eyes and rest my head on the edge of the desk.

"What's wrong with her now?" I heard Head Willie ask.

"Dunno, Boss. Still sick, I guess." That was Victor.

"Auntie!" Head Willie called. "Come here."

Seconds later, I heard Gloria enter, proceeded by her perfume. "What, Willie?"

"What's wrong with her? Has she been fed and watered, as we discussed?" Willie asked.

"Of course! Jerk chicken tonight—not too spicy, either. She is just a weakling, that's all. Not too bright, neither."

My head was yanked back by the hair. "What's wrong with you, Miss Phoebe?"

I gazed into Willie's eyes. "Sick," I whispered.

He released me and I let my head loll on my chest. "Never mind," he said. "Your condition will help make my point. Victor, have we the instruments ready?"

"Ready, Boss."

I cast a sideways glance at a long gleaming knife and a pair of pliers by the keyboard, but it was the sight of the hypodermic needle that hit me hardest. *Oh, shit. They were going to shoot me up?*

"Let us proceed, then. Jack, make the call."

"Yes, Boss." That must be one of the tech guys.

I hung my head listening as a digital dial tone rang several times followed by a click and another voice. "Hello? Hello?" That wasn't Noel or Toby.

There was a pause, one so fraught with tension that I heard Willie gasp. "Father?"

"Roger, is that you?"

I looked up, straight into the face of an older man with a fuzz of silver hair and glasses. His concern-filled gaze held mine.

"Is that you, Phoebe? Are you all right, my dear? We have been so worried."

I opened my mouth to speak but Willie pulled back my head and held a knife to my throat. "Where is Tobias and his 2IC?" he demanded. "It is to them I want to speak, not you! Get them before I slice her."

"Wait, stop this at once!" the elder Williams demanded. "Let that poor woman go! They are not here, either of them. They are out looking for her now."

"So contact them. Say that I'm going to turn Miss Phoebe here into a junkie if they don't do as I say."

"Roger, what are you doing, *what have you done?*"

"What do you think? She is my prisoner and so she will stay until I speak to Tobias and Noel! Call them immediately and tell him I hold her captive. Say that I will carve her up bit by bit and pump her full of my worst shit until I get what I want." I felt the knife break my skin and blood trickle down my neck.

"Stop that!" the older man said. "Son, what kind of monster have you become? Did your mother and I not give you all our love, did we not sacrifice our comforts to send you and your sister to university? You had everything you needed and more. You were our lives. Nothing else mattered to us but our family and our faith, and for this...for this, you have become a monster?"

Willie released me and straightened, shoving my chair away so he could step before the screen. "Do not start with me, Father," he said, shaking the knife at him. "I will not have it! You are a pathetic, sorry man who gives and gives but never takes. You let the church steal your money and your children the rest. Where has that gotten you? Tell me!

Look at me. You should be proud that I am rich and powerful while you are nothing!"

And then an older woman appeared on the screen. "Don't you dare speak to your father that way, Roger Williams! My Lord, but you are our shame—our only son a violent drug-dealing bully. Look at you, abusing innocent women! Some days I can hardly bear it." She place one hand on her chest, her eyes spilling tears. "I think my heart will break in two, Roger. Do you hear me? Can you hear it breaking now? How did I fail you, tell me that, son? What happened to my little boy?" And then she collapsed into sobs while her husband held her and glared over at Willie.

"Look what you are doing to your mother, Roger, the woman who brought you into the world and nursed your scrapes and comforted you when you were sick. Have you no shame?"

"Listen to you, Lee, the big holier than thou!" Gloria said, entering the fray. She nudged her nephew aside and bore down at the screen, hands on hips. "Why don't you see your son for the rich and powerful man he is instead if some little boy you can push around?"

"Oh, Gloria, Gloria. Why are you even still there?" her brother said. "My dear little sister."

"Dear little sister, my ass! Why am I here?" Gloria squealed, waving her diamond ring before the screen. "Because of this! I have everything I could ever want, that's why! All you ever did was make me feel bad for wanting beautiful things, but look at me now, lady of this mansion with pools and two private beaches and boats and cars. What do you have, Lee?"

As she went on to itemize more of her prized possessions, I pressed my toes against the tiles and rolled my chair back an inch. No one noticed. Even Victor stood transfixed as the family battle raged before him. One of the tech guys saw what I was doing but looked away. I budged back another inch, and then another and another, while Mr. and Mrs. Williams chastised Gloria with at least as much pain as they leveled at their son.

When I was almost at the door, I slipped from the chair and padded my bare feet across the den to the sliding door—locked, and once again my fiddling couldn't budge it. Needed a key, probably.

Forget that. I bolted for the hall, retracing the way I'd come toward the dude lounge.

It was a calculated risk. I was betting that the men inside the party room were either drunk or drugged and celebrating some victory or other while a skeleton crew kept watch—a skeleton crew that appeared to be posted elsewhere.

But as I approached the room, I realized that I had to be jumping from the frying pan into the fire. Men clustered in the hall outside. One had a woman backed into a corner while a little knot of guys stood around laughing and smoking.

"Hey!" one said, grabbing me as I tried slipping past. "Where you goin', gorgeous?" he asked, pulling me against him. His breath was so alcohol-laced it could have marinated my eyebrows. I tried to wiggle away but he held me tight. "Were you going dere, baby? I like you," he murmured into my ear as one hand roamed my butt and his groin ground against me.

A knee jab was so tempting right then but I played along. "I like you, too, big boy, but Vic told me to wait for him inside," I cooed, trying for the breathless Marilyn Monroe thing, which came out more like a wheeze.

The dude didn't notice. He just swore and released me. "Lucky bastard."

I escaped and dove inside the smoky room, now so dark and hazy I could barely see. The lights had been dimmed for maximum ambience and maybe even privacy, since half the bodies were naked and most were already paired up and getting it on. And the women were an international array—imports, I thought—most of whom seemed totally out of it, oblivious to what the men were doing to them.

I tried covering my nose against the drug smoke, hoping to keep my brain cells active, but it was hard enough staying balanced with all my limbs on call. There had to be at least fifteen guys in there and that many women. Shoving aside the pulsing bodies and navigating the human flesh took all my attention. It was the waft of fresh air blowing from across the room that kept me going.

An expanse of night sky was in my sights when I tripped, landing right on top of a coupling pair. The guy barely noticed, just bucked me off, sending me rolling onto the floor while the woman called out: "Gonna join us, honey?"

Then a voice bellowed into the room as the ceiling lights flooded the space. "Where's she at?"

Victor!

"Find dat woman!" he called.

"What one, Vic?"

"Her!"

"Dat her?" the woman cried, pointing to me.

I scrambled away on my hands and knees, heading for the door, ready to dash for the balcony, when a guy blocked my path. "You're not goin' nowhere, sugar."

Wrong. I leveled a kick to his groin, following up with a right hook that caught him squarely on the nose. Seconds later, I was bolting out onto the balcony and hanging a left while a tangle of muddled men tried to extricate themselves from their partners.

It was Victor I worried about. He was sober and furious, while the rest were semi-incapacitated. I heard him before I saw him, his footsteps beating on the deck as I flung chairs behind me and bolted past scattered couples. The deck lighting provided just enough illumination to keep me from tripping but I stayed focused dead ahead, aware of the seascape beyond but not daring to look.

My goal was to reach the place where Victor had held me over the balcony the first time, a destination that turned out to be much further away than I expected. I thought it would be just around the corner, that I'd see the lights of Willie's den, judging the spot from there, but the landscape of this balcony was all wrong. There was the pool, for one thing, a long narrow plunge pool empty but for a couple relaxing on the steps.

When I turned a corner for what I hoped would be the home stretch, I ran maybe twenty yards and hit a wall—literally. I spun around, my back to the concrete as Victor came striding toward me.

It struck me in a flash that I was on the wrong balcony on the wrong level. The stairs and route changes had turned me around. I could tell that I was too high up and that the sea seemed further off to the left rather than directly below.

Of course, Boss Willie wouldn't let his army loose in his living quarters. They had to be on the other side of the compound, maybe even in a separate interconnected building. Though the sea still sounded comfortingly close, it wasn't close enough.

I couldn't risk taking my eyes off Victor to scope it out. He was striding toward me with undisguised satisfaction on his hardened face. "Where you tink you goin', bitch?"

Ah, there was the question—if only I knew. But one thing was clear: I'd rather die than fall into his clutches again.

He slowed down, big arms spread on either side of his body, watching my face as I watched his. The whole time I was measuring, calculating, calling up everything my martial arts trainer had ever told me. *Always use the element of surprise; always aim to incapacitate first in order to escape second; remember that a man can protect his groin, but rarely his shins or his nose, but his groin is still the most vulnerable.*

With Brenda's words in my head, I waited until he was a foot away before springing forward to knee his gonads. His shocked face was a photo op waiting to happen, but that only gave me time to kick again, this time in the shins, before sending a right hook to his jaw. With my bare feet and sore shoulder, the impact wasn't half of what I needed but he still doubled over in shock and rage, which gave me the precious seconds required to clutch the railing and leap over the other side.

I meant it when I said I'd rather die. Still, my best scenario would be to drop straight into the sea and swim away into the moonlight. That didn't happen. Instead, I fell directly onto the crown of a palm, clinging to the fronds as the tree bent toward the ground. For a few terrifying seconds, I thought the thing would snap in two or, worse, spring back and fling me against the house, but the tree had already taken a beating in the storm and just sagged onto the rocks.

Rocks, I didn't need rocks, I needed sea! But scramblers can't be choosers, so I started climbing over the coral boulders heading toward the sound of waves.

I don't know how long I carried on—maybe minutes or only seconds. The shouting told me they were gaining and that silver moonlight sent me into high relief. But desperate women do desperate things and I was oblivious to my scraped and probably bleeding feet, to the crazy business of struggling over coral rock to an unknown destination, even to the crack and ping of bullets ricocheting off the rocks. Maybe Willie figured that an escaped Miss Phoebe may as well be a dead Miss Phoebe.

I turned, seeing flashlight beams as the men climbed after me, but I realized that I'd come farther than I thought. I'd made it to the point already.

Swinging back to face the sea, I risked standing up. Now I could tell that I was on a promontory about twelve feet above the water and that the waves weren't furious exactly, just ebbing and flowing with occasional rogues sending plumes into the air. It felt like home, only multiple degrees warmer.

"Phoebe McCabe, you stop now or you will be dead! Do you hear me! You will not escape!" That was Big Willie's voice over a loud speaker. A shot hit stone no more than a foot away, spraying my legs with shards of coral rock.

That was it. I took the plunge.

15

I expected to hit the rocks, jumping feetfirst for that very reason—
better to break a leg than smash a skull—but instead, I kept sinking. Down, down, down I went, beams of moonlight shimmering
through the shifting surface. It was otherworldly and beautiful, the
water slipping across my skin cool and soothing even though my abra-
sions stung. Like a mother applying antiseptic to a cut, it was a good
kind of sting. Deep in Mother Sea's arms, I imagined living forever
but, in reality, I knew I'd probably last less than a minute. I needed air.

Kicking upward, I broke the surface. The Willies hadn't reached
the edge yet, which meant I still had time to disappear. Powering away
from the rocks, I pulled in every scrap of remaining energy to swim
against the current and around the point. The water churned with
storm flotsam—a tangle of leaves and fronds, carpets of wood and plastic, which I had to plow through. I tore off the nightgown while
clinging to a piece of wood, since the fabric only entangled my limbs.
In nothing but a bra and panties, I powered on.

Somehow I made it to the other side where I found myself in a tiny
cove surrounded by a ridge of rock. Ahead, I could just see a crescent
of sand backed against a fringe of palms.

The shouting sounded further away, which I hoped meant that the men were searching the water around the point, thinking that poor little stupid Phoebe had fallen to her watery grave. Maybe the floating nightgown might encourage that nonsense.

My feet touched the sandy bottom. *Never ever underestimate the power of a furious woman.* Did I remember that right? I didn't care. It hit me like a mantra just then, and I repeated that line over and over as I pushed against the tide. When I reached the beach, it was all I could do to drag myself up into the shelter of the foliage.

I lay shivering on a layer of fronds and plastic bottles, trying to decide what to do the next. The men may not be in the best state for tracking me but there was still Victor. And Gloria, not that she'd think that was her job. I had to keep moving.

Which way would I head? Away, was all I knew. Dragging myself to my feet, I plunged deeper into the foliage until I broke through onto another, much bigger beach and stopped. Ahead, a little moonlight-limned boat bobbed in the waves close to shore, with another half-submerged nearby.

I plowed through the water up to my waist. The name of a resort marked it as a storm runaway but the tarp covering was still secured. In minutes, I had the tarp off to reveal a perfect little sailboat complete with intact sails tucked into the bottom along with oars and a life preserver—a little tourist pack complete with laminated sailing instructions.

Flipping the torn anchor rope inside, I turned the prow into the waves, and hefted myself in. My shoulders groaned as I shoved the oars into the surf and pushed the little boat against the waves to reach open water. Every muscle screamed in protest as the waves slapped the prow.

I had no idea where I was heading. Maybe there were reefs nearby —hell, there *must* be reefs nearby; the coral rock told me that much— but I had no choice but to sail blindly.

When I was far enough away from shore, I hoisted the sail, thrilled to see her swell in the wind and to know my little craft was going places. Here was my element—the sea, the wind, a boat. I grew up on water, respected it without fear because I knew I could handle myself in almost any circumstance. Besides, I was escaping prison and was probably slightly drug-addled.

Shivering even in the humid air with one hand gripping the rudder, I settled into my bliss. I'd just sail and sail, hoping that another boat or a plane might spy me or that I'd find a town or a resort I could dive into. Though there was a rescue flare in the boat, I couldn't risk firing it off and announcing my whereabouts to the Willies.

Really, I thought I'd made it, relatively speaking, until two things happened simultaneously. First, I saw the unmistakable shape of reefs in shallow water dead ahead, and second, I heard the buzz of a speedboat far behind me.

I swung around. Shit. A boat was zipping toward me from around the point and now I had no place to sail, since the reef barricaded me from the open sea. Maybe I could navigate back closer to the shore but I'd never outrun a speedboat. And if I kept the boat aimed toward the reef, I might be able to ride a wave for a minute but would soon run aground —the tide was out, the jagged reefs exposed. The moonlight enhanced everything—me, the boat, the reef. I was the proverbial sitting duck.

Then I heard another boat coming from somewhere. They'd soon surround me. I turned the boat so that the sail shielded my body. Snatching the flare gun still in its plastic sheath, I shoved it into my bra and dropped over the side.

I swam directly for the reef. Once I climbed onto the coral, I planned to clamber along until I could descend into a pool between the formations, thinking that the keel of a speedboat wouldn't get very far. Sure, they'd come after me but I'd find a place to hide, dive deeper if I had to, navigate around the reefs, and maybe stay alive a bit longer. Or drown. Death by drowning would be preferable to death by Willie.

I made it past the surf crashing against the coral and onto the first ridge, picking my way over the sharp formations, oblivious to my feet. The coral seemed mostly dead, so at least I wasn't stepping on some living colony. Still, the sound of the speedboat crashing into the reef behind me made me nuts. *Bastards. Show some respect!*

Though I didn't slow down to look, I sensed that at least three men were climbing out on the reef after me with more on the way.

"You stop, bitch, before I blow de brains out!"

Victor—I'd recognize his gentle words anywhere. "Go to hell!" I screamed.

A bullet hit my leg, sending me spinning backward. I managed to topple to the left into a sandy pool between the formations. My feet touched the bottom as I watched the moonlight turn my blood into a stream of inky black. Vaguely I wondered if the reef sharks would get me before the Willies. Funny what we think of when we're on our way out.

I had just enough energy left to pull out the flare gun and point it to the first bastard to reach me. Victor. Though I sensed many others scrambling forward—more boats, more shouting, more gunshots—I only had eyes for him. He now leveled his gun at me, and bared his teeth. But I fired first.

There was a blaze of neon pink as I dipped below the surface and then everything went black.

🍃 16 🍃

For one horrible moment, I thought I was back on the bed in Willieville. Though still warm and humid, the air felt different, *smelled* different. A soft jasmine-scented breeze billowed the mosquito netting around the bed, only I didn't recall there being netting. And then I heard crickets loud enough to be chirping inside my head.

I sat up. Everything ached as I shoved away the netting and stared into the room. French doors were flung open to the first break of dawn. A wad of bandages and a jar of antiseptic sat on a nightstand nearby and, across the room, a pair of long jean-clad legs extended from the shadows.

Maybe I was hallucinating. Maybe I was gripped by a fever still. Trying to force my brain out of this dream-state into reality wasn't happening. I needed to move, yet once my feet touched down on the tiled floor, such a stab of agony followed that I stifled a cry. Okay, so the pain was real, but everything else seemed totally divorced from my recent experience.

I should be dead. Maybe I was.

I gazed down at my arms covered in scratches and then past the knee-length nightie to my bandaged leg. So, that explained the worst pain. The gunshot I remembered. Everything right up to the flare came tumbling back in complete nightmare clarity but nothing thereafter. Where was I?

Across the room, those legs shifted slightly. I winced my way to the other side of the table to see their owner fully. He was slumped deep into the armchair, one arm cradling his head, the other stretched along the armrest. Strands of dark hair curled across his forehead above eyes that even while closed seemed sunken with fatigue.

"Noel!"

He sprang awake, jumping to his feet while simultaneously pulling a pistol from somewhere. My hands flew up as he came fully alert. "Phoebe! Oh, hell. I thought they'd come back." Setting the gun on the table, he took me by the shoulders. "Phoebe, Phoebe. I'm sorry, love. Are you all right?"

But I had collapsed into tears by then. The sight of him plus the gun just did me in. Weak, lily-livered creature that I was, all I could do was sob against his chest.

"I'm sorry. Oh, Phoebe," he said, stroking my hair.

"This is how you live now?" I sniffed. "Ready to shoot the first person who wakes you up?"

"No, ready to shoot the first person who tries to hurt you again. Nothing's going to happen to you while I'm here."

I buried my face into his chest, inhaling his spicy scent. "I thought I'd never see you again," I whispered.

"I would have torn up the Caribbean palm by palm until I found you, no matter what the cost. When I heard that bastard had captured you, I was ready to storm the fortress—almost did, in fact. Then we heard that you'd escaped—thank God. The Willies didn't know what trouble they were taking on by capturing Phoebe McCabe."

"Yeah, I'm a real kick-ass when I can stand up straight and don't upchuck every meal."

He laughed, then suddenly sobered. "The doc says you have an infection causing a fever, been partially choked, hit by a heavy object, and, more recently, had your leg grazed by a bullet. Am I missing anything? I've been torn up thinking what they did to you—might have done to you—but you're safe now. Still, I could kick myself for sending that postcard."

I pulled away to look up at him. "What, and never see me again?"

"I would have found a way."

"Well, you weren't doing a great job of that in the past few months, were you?"

We both laughed. "I guess not," he agreed. "I didn't want to give Interpol too much fun at my expense. Here, let's get you back to bed—and ordinarily I would give that the wickedest of connotations, but the doctor says that you are to rest, no exceptions."

He picked me up in his arms while I just stared into those deep hazel eyes wanting so much to kiss him that I almost had to bite my lip.

"Are Max and the others okay?" I asked as he carried me over.

"Father was with me when we surrounded those bastards on the reef. He's still got what it takes, I'll say that much for him. He and Peaches helped cover me while I pulled you out of the water. Phoebe," he said, stopping to cast me his sternest look, "you could have been blinded by firing off that flare so close."

"And would have been dead if I hadn't. Anyway, I flipped back into the water with my eyes closed." And because I couldn't stand it any longer, I brought my lips to his.

What followed was a long, deep kiss, one not for the fainthearted since I can't remember breathing during most of it. He laid me across the covers without removing his lips from mine and took his time enjoying every second, one hand gently outlining my body until he touched something that hurt. My yelp made him pull away.

"Damn, I'm sorry," he said, holding up his hands. "It's way too soon for that."

I held out my arms. "Never too soon. Think I traveled through the jungle to lie around in a bed by myself? Come back. It's just my temple and my leg you have to be careful of."

"Plus every inch in between. The doc says you have to rest," he told me.

"The doc obviously doesn't know what I really need."

But then came a knock on the door and in walked a couple who looked familiar, though I couldn't immediately place their faces.

"Phoebe, may I introduce my good friends, Lee and Barbara Williams," Noel said.

"Roger's parents. We met, sort of," I said, sitting up. "Hi. Nice to meet you both properly."

"Dearest Phoebe," Mr. Williams said, taking my hand. "We are so relieved that you escaped our monster of a son, and we do apologize for all the trauma he put you through."

"It's not your fault," I said. "The sins of the sons are not visited on the fathers—or mothers."

Barbara stepped forward, shaking her head. "And yet we bear them in our hearts, nonetheless. How are you feeling, my dear?" She was a short broad woman encased in a tight dress, her hair curling to her shoulders, her face alive with a broad smile—Roger's smile, I realized, or at least it could have been his smile had he worn it with his mother's spirit.

"Much better, thanks, just a little sore in places." I caught Noel's eyes as his lips quirked one of those heart-flipping smiles. What I really wanted to say was, that now that I was among those I loved, nothing else mattered. Forget the recent past, forget the battered body.

The whir of a motorized wheelchair prompted Barbara and Lee to step aside as my brother zoomed up to my bed. I barely noticed his red Zeus beard as I slipped off the covers and into his arms, breaking down into tears again. I couldn't help myself. "Toby," I whispered as he hugged me hard. "I can't believe I'm really here with you again."

"I know, I know. I'm sorry, sis," he said, patting my back. "We'll catch up later."

"All right, my boys, it is time to let our Phoebe rest," Lee said. "Her body has been through the war and the only thing that will help now, except for your love, of course, is complete peace. Away with you both while I examine her and change those dressings."

"Aye-aye, Dr. Williams," Toby said, helping me back on the bed before putting his chair in reverse. "We will have plenty of time to catch up later, Phoebe. Love you, girl."

"I love you, too," I said, trying to arrest my sniveling. "Dr. Williams?" I asked, turning to Lee.

"Dr. Williams, yes, family practitioner now retired, but you must call me Lee."

"And me Barbara," his wife added. "We don't abide by formalities here."

"Indeed we don't," Lee said with a smile, "but nevertheless I shall play formal physician here and dispense orders. Your body has been through a great trial and now you must let it heal." He sent a pointed look to Noel. "And while you heal, others should rest. That means you, son."

"He hasn't slept properly for days," Barbara told me. "We couldn't pry him from your bedside—your brother and Max, either—that is, until I convinced them that a crowded bedroom was mighty unhealthy. They took turns from then on. Now shoo, all of you."

My men backed out, casting me long looks before Barbara joined them and shut the door. I leaned back against the pillows and studied Roger Williams's father, who smiled at me as he began removing the bandage from my leg. He was a handsome man, his silver hair like a nimbus against his mahogany skin.

"We have been most concerned about you, Phoebe," he said with his head down over my leg. Other than the deep voice, there was little family resemblance between father and son that I could tell. Maybe a murderous life changes a man's face, and maybe Roger could have been like this lean man with the warm eyes and gentle touch. What a fool for not emulating his parents.

"Where are we, Lee, and how did you come to be here with my brother and Noel?"

"Ah, now there's a story," he said while peeling away the bandage and dropping it into a pail beside him. "Indeed it is, though it will sound simple on the surface. I was a practicing physician on the mainland when I was called to tend a young man on this little island two years ago. We knew that the isle was heavily guarded but did not know why."

"So, this *is* their hideout."

"Yes, indeed, but I was unaware of what kind of hideout. There have always been rumors about the island. Long ago it belonged to a famous Hollywood star who purchased it for his escape and then we heard that two men had bought it to reinstate a resort. That it was of great interest to my son, who was already dabbling in the drug trade—that is what a degree in economics gets you apparently—told us something."

"You thought that whoever lived here was also distributing drugs?"

"Or purchasing them. Later, I would understand that the story was not so simple but had no idea at the time. Then one night I was called to the island to tend a young man who had been badly injured in an explosion."

"Noel. In Orvieto."

"Yes, I believe so. Were you involved in that?"

"I was."

"In any case, I made frequent visits after that and came to know both Noel and Tobias. We all became family—there is no truer word for it. Perhaps we each offer what the other needs—me, a son or two, and they a father, and perhaps a mother, too. Though I don't approve of what they do exactly, I do appreciate the men they are, despite it all. I admire them, in truth. Well, I did. In any case, there is a bond."

"But Roger implied that Toby stole you from him."

Lee shook his head sadly. "Oh, yes, he would, for he sees the world through a very narrow viewfinder these days, my son. The fact that Barbara, Penelope, and I will not align ourselves with his horrific and reprehensible lifestyle makes us traitors in his eyes. We do not see money and power as the only goal in life, making us pitiful in his eyes. He chooses not to hold his own actions responsible for our alienation, but prefers to blame your brother. That is so much easier to accept. I am about apply antiseptic, my dear. Hold on."

I managed not to squeal. "Is Penelope your daughter?" I said between clenched teeth.

"Indeed she is and the light of our lives she is, too." He smiled. "Now, hang on while I replace the bandage and then I shall give you another shot of antibiotics plus something for the pain."

"What about Gloria?"

A shadow crossed his face. "Gloria, my older sister, cares not what

Roger does as long as he keeps her in the manner in which she feels she deserves. Should she ever pull away the veil that blinds her and sees what she has truly become, I fear what she will do to herself. My sister is not stable. There. Are you ready for the needle?"

"Sure, shoot away." I regretted my choice of words the moment I said them. "So, we're on an island," I said as I turned on my side to ready for the stab.

"Indeed we are, and a lovelier place on earth you will never find. Don't worry, Phoebe, we are well guarded here."

⚜

MOONLIGHT WAS FLOODING THROUGH THE SCREENED DOORS BY THE time I awoke. I must have slept for hours. Whatever was in that painkiller had to have had a narcotic component since not only was I feeling no pain, but a mild euphoria sang in my veins.

Which only increased when I rolled over onto my side and bumped into a bare back. A warm tropical night, a half-naked man? If this was some dream state, I was all in. Running my hand across his skin, all my imaginative flights over the last long months came pouring back. I was no longer alone. The man I loved occupied the same slice of earth. And to think I had to fly halfway across the world just to come home.

He moaned as he turned toward me.

"Am I dreaming you?" I whispered, stroking his chest.

"Pretty certain I'm real, Phoebe, unless you want to launch a philosophical discussion right now."

"Mmm..." I tasted his lips while my hand explored southward. "Maybe later. Right now, my mind's focused on less cerebral matters and...I'm busy."

He grinned, the moonlight illuminating every feature as if we had a light shining right by the bed. "Phoebe." He stroked my hair. "You'll never get back to sleep."

"Good—last thing on my mind." I rolled over on top of him, only wincing once when my leg pressed against the mattress. My hips were doing their own thing, my heart accelerating by the second. "I need medicine," I whispered, looking down at him. "You may have to help me out of this nightie, but after that I think I can hold my own."

He gave me a wicked grin. "Oh, I believe I can do better than that."

⚜

I FELL INTO A DEEP SLEEP AFTERWARD, AND WHEN I AWOKE AGAIN he was still beside me, only this time sitting up on the edge of the bed. It was still dark outside but my heart felt incredibly light.

"Noel," I murmured, reaching out to him.

He took my hand and held tight. "Phoebe, love, I've got so much I must tell you."

"Hmm...right now? What's wrong with more body language? You were very fluent a while ago," I whispered, drawing his head down to kiss me and his free hand toward my naked body.

He laughed, pulling away. "Because what I need to say requires actual words."

"Sounds serious," I said, propping myself up on my elbows.

"It is and we're running out of time."

"How so?"

"You need to speak to your brother, then you'll understand. Meanwhile, I must get to work."

"On me? I'm waiting."

He laughed again. "Oh, how I wish, but not on you this time, sadly. I have a few other things I need, rather than want, to do."

"But it's still nighttime."

He took me by the shoulders. "Just listen. I've slipped a piece of paper into the lining of that carpetbag pet of yours. It's a coded list of clues to the whereabouts of all the art I have secreted around Europe. Keep it safe. Tell nobody, understand? I'm serious. I'll get the cipher to you as soon as I'm able, but for now guard that list. Better still, commit it to memory and destroy the thing. You'll understand why soon enough."

"What's going on?" I said, suddenly wide awake and alarmed.

But he was now getting dressed and I was temporarily distracted by the view of his jeans being pulled up over his torso. Talk about the total eclipse of the sun.

"We'll talk later. I have to go now." He stepped back to the bed while still zippering his fly and gave me a long, deep kiss before pulling away and jogging out the screen door.

I just sat there, dazed. What had just happened, besides the incredibly hot loving? Why was he deserting me when we'd only just reconnected? I needed much more than that, and preferably all at once.

Sitting up, I noticed a banana plus a couple of rolls wrapped in plastic beside a bottle of water on the nightstand. I swilled back the water, devoured the banana plus one of the rolls. Thus fortified, I sat there for a few minutes savoring how much better I felt—more alive, almost feverish with life force. Whatever was scribbled on that paper could wait.

Here I was ensorcelled in a kind of paradise among those I cared about, all my dreams manifested. Maybe it was the painkillers or maybe I was simply love-drunk, but I intended to float along on this cushion of bliss for as long as I could.

My first few halting steps took me to the screen doors, which I shoved open and stepped out onto a little ground-level patio. A silvered garden spread around me and, beyond that, the sea glowed in the moonlight. Warm trade winds cooled the humidity and the lights of cottages twinkled through the foliage. It was nothing less than magic.

Padding back inside, I snatched the first thing I found that could cover my nightdress, shoved my feet into a pair of flip-flops, and returned to the garden. From there, I hobbled along a path threading through the fronds. Smiling, I brushed against night jasmine as I carried along the path. The grounds were so tidy and lovingly tended, all signs of the hurricane swept away. I almost felt as if I were floating.

Soon I found myself on a little knoll overlooking a cove where boats bobbed at their moorings. Lights indicated that each one was manned and soon I realized that they formed a circle, possibly encircling the island. A figure patrolled one of the larger vessels, the silhouette of a gun unmistakable as he strolled back and forth on deck. The island was surrounded by boats. How sweet.

By now I was exhausted and my leg throbbed a bit but my brain was no less grounded. The solar-light paths lit the grounds like fairy fires and seemed to go on and on, and though my urge to explore remained undaunted, I didn't have the energy. I was about to sit down on a garden seat when I heard somebody approaching through the trees.

"Declare yourself or I'll shoot," she ordered.

"Phoebe McCabe," I cried, holding up my hands. "Don't make me die from friendly fire. Is that you, Peaches?" Like I wouldn't recognize her voice anywhere.

"Oh, shit—Phoebe! What are you doing prancing around here in the dark?"

I watched as the long legs stepped out of the foliage. Wearing shorts and a luminous orange vest over a halter top but not much else, she looked like Naomi Campbell playing night jogger.

"I'm not exactly prancing and I was just taking in the air."

"You could end up taking in bullets, if you're not careful. We wear these reflective vests when walking here at night so guards like me don't tink we're Willies and shoot you full of holes."

"Charming," I muttered.

She stopped and gave me a big grin. "But it sure is good to see you, Phoebe. Oh, hell, girl, I was so worried about you!" Then she hugged me hard, and let me just say that being hugged by a woman whose bust just reaches the top of your head is weird.

"I was worried about you, too, but you, Joe, and Max got away," I said, falling back. Peaches caught me before I stumbled downhill.

"Yeah. There. You okay? We made it to the cove, no prob, and the boat was waiting for us, as planned. We thought you'd end up there eventually, too, but it didn't happen. Then Joe found your backpack washed up on de beach and we knew you were in trouble. That's when the Captain and Noel went nuts."

I lowered myself down onto the marble seat and pulled the robe closer around my arms. It only took a bit of exertion to drive home how weak I actually was. My hands smoothed across the fabric and stopped: I recognized quality silk when I felt it—thick, fluid crepe de chine, to be specific. Then I held up my bum leg to inspect and found a gourmet flip-flop with a hydrangea flower feature dangling at the end of my foot. "What the hell am I wearing?"

"Couture, dahling. What do you tink?" Peaches waved her hand and struck a pose. "I didn't take you for the type but they sure be yours. Mom found them in your suitcase when she unpacked for you. You saving them for a special occasion or someting? I'd have thought that being reunited with your hottie qualified there."

"Nicolina."

"Come again?"

"Never mind. Where do Max, Toby, and Noel sleep?"

Peaches jerked her head toward the path. "Max is staying with Noel in the main house, same as you, and the Captain has his own digs attached."

"Why do they call him the Captain?"

"Because he's de boss."

"I suppose." But it left me unsettled, though I didn't know why.

"Come on. We've got to get you back in bed or Dad will have my neck." And with that, she simply picked me up in her arms like so much laundry and launched down the path.

"Dad?" I asked her as we bounced along. "You're Penelope?"

"Yeah, but everyone who doesn't want a fat lip calls me Peaches, 'cept Mom and Dad, of course. Do I look like a Penelope to you?"

"No, but you sure as hell don't look like a Peaches, either."

She laughed. "It's a nickname my daddy gave me when I was a sprog. I love my fruits, indeed I do."

She took a different path. "Where are we going?"

"Just want to show you something first."

We broke through the fronds to a skim of beach. Across the water no more than a hundred yards away sat a tiny island linked by an equally small bridge. Peaches bounded across the span to the center point before lowering my feet to the surface. "What do you think?" she asked, spreading her arms.

For a moment I focused on what looked to be a child's play castle just visible through the palms on the tiny isle. A turreted tower glowed ghostly in the moonlight. "It looks like something out of a fairy tale."

"Never mind that, look at de bridge."

Then a man with a rifle slung over his shoulder came to the edge of the water and waved at Peaches. "Don't worry about him, neither," she said. "That's just Cecil. He's on guard duty there tonight. It's de bridge I want you to look at, de bridge."

My gaze dropped to my feet. I didn't know what to say. It was a bridge—sturdy, functional. "It's cool," I said. "I feel totally safe standing here, and I love the graceful curve of the span."

Peaches's grin flashed in the moonlight. "That's what I want you to feel. This is my bridge. I designed and built it and, trust me, a tank could roll over this thing and it wouldn't budge."

"Wow. I forgot that you are an engineer."

"Structural engineer but I almost took architecture before I switched, and making bridges and other structures is one of the tings I love to do more than anything."

"Really?"

"Really," she said, picking me up. "And if I weren't a gun-toting pseudo-bandit, I'd be flying all over de world building amazing tings— dat is, if anyone would hire me. I always wanted to see the world."

"You should never give up on your dream. I don't care how glib that sounds, it's still true," I told her as we bounced along.

"Tell dat to my bank account. Right now I'll settle for trying to do some good in the world."

"And working for my brother fulfills that?"

"Not exactly." She didn't speak for a moment, then she added: "It used to, sort of. Then tings changed." I was getting used to her Jamaican accent melding into Colonial English.

"Changed how?" We were bouncing along, every glimpse more gorgeous than the next—the cottages through the trees, the flowers, the pools, the ocean.

"They're sinking, Phoebe, that's all I can say."

"Sinking how?"

"Just sinking. You got to ask them about it and make them be truthful."

Urging someone to be truthful had never been my strong point. Instead, apparently I had a gift for inspiring subterfuge, half-truths, and outright lies.

❧ 17 ❧

The next morning, Dr. Lee gave me the thumbs-up. "The leg is healing nicely and I see no secondary infection. The antibiotics are clearly working, which is very good," he said, nodding to himself as if he was enormously pleased with his assessment. "I've applied a waterproof bandage, of which we have plenty."

"Does this mean I can take a shower and get dressed?" Here I was reunited with my man and, once again, I looked like a wounded desperado. Not a victim but a survivor, I reminded myself, but no less battered.

"Proceed with caution, my dear. You are still not fighting fit. A shower would be fine, though I'd prefer that you remained resting for a while longer. Perhaps you could read a book for a few days? There is an excellent library on the property, one to which we have all contributed, and I could recommend some of my favorites."

"Thank you. Maybe I'll take a browse later on. Do you spend all your time on the island these days?"

"For the most part, yes, now that I'm retired. Every Sunday Barbara and I take a boat to Port Antonio across the way there to attend church and to visit friends, but otherwise this is my home now. Your brother offered to build us a church here but it would not be fitting."

"Why wouldn't it be fitting?"

"I could not ask a man of the faith to visit this island in light of present circumstances."

"I don't understand."

He shook his head. "And it is not my story to tell. Good day to you, my dear. I hope you will enjoy a most magnificent day."

"Is that like 'don't worry, be happy'?"

He laughed. "Very close!"

"I hope to do some knitting."

His gaze followed mine through the open door to the patio where somebody, presumably Barbara, had hung my yarn and mangled project up to dry. Until I washed the sand and mud from the strands, my knitting remained at a standstill.

"Ah, you have a hobby, I see. Very good."

"Not a hobby, more like a passion. Unfortunately, my knitting took a nosedive in the river but I'm hoping for a complete recovery."

Nearly everything in the backpack had suffered some kind of water damage, including my beloved carpetbag, also drying in the sun. My phone was simply dead and what I had by way of clothes—a sweater and an extra pair of jeans—had disappeared, hopefully into the closet I had yet to investigate.

"Well, I shall check on you later, then, Phoebe. Good day to you for now."

"Wait, please, Lee."

He stopped at the door, and turned.

"Is everything is all right around here?"

"In regards to?"

"In regards to this island, my brother, Noel..."

"Ah, yes," he said, gazing down. "Well, as I said previously, it is best that you ask them, Phoebe."

"But they don't appear to be around to ask." Or at least no one had come visiting while I was awake.

He smiled. "Oh, but they will be here tonight. For now, Noel is off doing scouting duties—this is his day, I believe, and he is especially concerned that our defenses may be compromised after the fracas. As for Tobias, he can't be far. He may be on his yacht, but I think not. I heard him say that he would remain close by. No matter, everyone will be present at dinnertime. Barbara is planning a family reunion dinner when we shall all raise a glass to present company. I am quite looking forward to it." And with that he smiled and left.

Once again I was supposed to wait all day to see Noel? That's what my life had become: periods of restless stasis followed by extreme acts of hunt and survival. At least I had been (sort of) reunited with both him and my brother here on this sliver of paradise, even if I couldn't immediately see either.

Something felt wrong. Surely Noel could find somebody else to switch duty days with? He must have thought I'd be sleeping all day. That had to be it. I needed to get dressed and track Toby and Max down. Really, this was unbearable. My soaring sense of well-being suddenly crashed.

Hobbling to the closet, I pulled back the curtain and stared at the swath of glorious textiles hanging on padded hangers, recognizing the hydrangea and Majorca pieces I wish-listed from Dolce & Gabbana but little else. There were many more gourmet pieces hanging there than what I could ever dream of owning.

Nicolina, what have you done? I fingered a silk sleeve. She had bought far more than what was on my silly list, and certainly more than what was needed to fool Rupert, if that was the plan. This new wardrobe had to be twenty times more than my clothing budget for a decade. A quick calculation rang up an estimate of close to fifteen thousand dollars.

And yet I still didn't have a thing to wear. Traipsing around in a silk Majorcan-designed sheath dress seemed more lunching-on-the-Amalfi than limping around this island fortress. I settled for the Majorcan bathing suit and matching silk cover-up and headed for the shower.

Standing there under the flood of water washing my hair with piña-colada-scented shampoo hit me with an intense memory of the time years ago when I first met Noel in Bermuda. He had filled out a wetsuit better than any man I'd known and we'd shared many fraught, often wonderful, but mostly adrenaline-fueled moments in the years that followed. I could count the time I'd spent with him in days, not weeks. Damn, but I yearned for him now. So why the hell wasn't he with me?

A few moments later, decked in my couture bathing suit, my hair a mass of unruly tendrils, I stepped into the room and nearly bumped into Max.

"Planning on a swim?" he asked, a vision of the slightly reddened tourist.

We exchanged one of our superhugs, while I cautioned him as to where and where not to squeeze.

"Ouch, careful. That's enough. Back away now."

He laughed, stepping back.

"Not exactly, to answer your question," I said. "But I come equipped with a designer wardrobe with nary a pair of capris or jeans in sight. Where's your sunscreen?"

"What sunscreen? Too hot for jeans, by the way." He indicated the pair of long shorts he sported. "Compliments of one of the island lads, but you can blame your brother for the Hawaiian shirt."

I grinned. "He still loves those things? But I'm envious. These clothes are incredible—and I never, ever thought to own anything this magnificent—but they just don't fit in here."

"Nicolina pulled another fast one on you, did she?"

"She's bent on showering me with expensive gifts."

"Proper thing, darlin'. You deserve it. Feeling better?"

"Yes, better," I said, towel-drying my hair. "How about you? How has the father-son reunion been going?"

Max gazed toward the screened door. "Well, it's moving along. It's not like I can undo the errors of my past in a couple of days, but Noel's been trying to give me a chance, and I've been trying to let things take their time." He turned back to me. "He's changed, Phoebe."

I paused. "How?"

"Wiser, sadder, maybe. I can't put a finger on it. On one hand he seems like the same lad, but in other ways not."

I lowered the towel. "Obviously. Max, you haven't seen him in years and in that time he's become a hunted man. Of course he's changed."

Max ran a hand through his thick mane. "Yes, you're right, darlin'—

of course he's changed. I just remember him as the angry young buck with a bone to pick."

"But now he's evolved. Like father, like son."

"And he seems to have a lot on his mind, not surprising, I guess."

"Did you find out anything about the Raphael?"

"Nothing. He's very evasive. I did ask, but he just says it turned out to be a forgery."

I met his eyes. "And you don't believe him?"

"Let's put it this way: I don't expect him to trust me yet."

"And Toby?"

"And Toby's something else again—Captain Firebeard, my foot. Sorry, Phoeb. I know he's your brother but that guy is as big a pain in the neck as he was as a kid."

I stared at him. "I don't remember him being a pain in the neck."

"No? You were pretty young when Toby, your dad, and I were trea- sure hunting around Nova Scotia. Anyway, he's not going to be any more forthcoming with me than he ever was. Don't forget he hid things from all of us in the end."

I sighed. It was true: my brother had been holding secrets from me for as long as I could remember. Why did I think that now, with so much at stake, things would be different?

"Look, darlin'," Max added, "forget that for now. Have you had breakfast?"

"Peaches delivered toast and fruit a while ago. That'll do. And I can't forget about this, ever. Whatever Toby and Noel have stashed here has attracted the worst kind of attention, plus it will only be a matter of days before Rupert tracks us down and maybe Interpol, too. Where is Toby, anyway?"

"I'll escort you to him," he said, offering his arm.

I laughed. "Just let me finish dressing first. Wait outside." And with that I finished my bathing-suit-and-matching-silk-robe-couture look, tied my hair into a bushy ponytail, shoved my feet into the world's most expensive flip-flops, and joined him outside my room.

"Can you walk?" he asked as I tucked my hand into his arm.

"I can limp just fine, thank you, and—wow—don't my feet look fetching? Those flowers just set off the whole look."

"For a woman who's just been through the mill, you look pretty damn good, Phoebe."

That wasn't quite true but I appreciated the gallantry. Besides, a few steps further down the hall and I was so busy taking in the house that everything else was forgotten.

"Wow," I commented as we entered a spacious columned room overlooking a large turquoise swimming pool. "This isn't what I expected. It's like a resort."

"Used to be a resort and, before that, the main lounge for Heston Finn—you know, the silver-screen actor?—to entertain his Hollywood friends. That was back in 1920s, remember, so the toppies back then were still trying to out-trump Hearst's glamorous digs at San Simeon."

"But why here?"

"Finn must have decided that a Caribbean hideaway was just the thing. He bought the island while he was filming *Beauties and Buccaneers* off the coast here. Then a resort took it over decades later but eventually went bust and the place fell to ruin."

"So it's definitely on the proverbial map."

"Oh, yes. Hard to hide. There are five en-suite bedrooms in the main house and about ten cottages spread across this main island and the islet yonder. A few follies, too. Finn was a romantic sod—liked to woo the ladies in true Hollywood settings."

"That explains the little turret thing I saw last night. My point about it being on the map is that it's not exactly a *hideaway*. Everybody knows about it."

"Hidden in plain sight. Apparently, everybody thinks there's another resort being constructed here. When Toby bought it," Max continued, "he was bidding against a big resort chain but Toby outbid them."

"Outbid them?" I made him stop. "Where'd he get that kind of money?"

"I don't know. Toby hit it rich with that software company of his, didn't he?"

"He did—past tense. As far as I know, that company and all its assets closed after he became a hunted man. Unless he's incredibly savvy with investments, I don't see how those funds could sustain him for long." Especially if renovating and guarding this place was part of his current lifestyle. "Let's find him."

"I'll take you to him now, but I'll warn you, you're in for another surprise, darlin'."

"Why?"

"Just wait for it. We'll compare notes after."

So we traveled the length of the house, passing housekeepers and groundsmen, and even a peacock that had wandered in from the lawn, until we reached an elevator.

"Peacocks?" I asked.

"Left over from the resort days. Everybody treats them like pets here. Had one roosting by my window last night—screeched like a ghost on fire."

"And all these worker bees?"

"Don't know whether they're for show or whether Tobias likes to be well-tended. I'm guessing the latter."

We entered a slick glass-and-steel elevator.

"This thing doesn't look vintage 1920s," I commented as we rose three floors up, occasional portholes blinking by in hues of turquoise and sky blue.

"State of the art," Max remarked, keeping his eyes averted.

The door swept open onto a round glass room like the top of a lighthouse, with 360-degree views of the island. Flooded in sunshine, every window framing the glorious Caribbean, the sight took my breath away. "Oh," I managed.

"Quite a perspective, hey, Phoebe?" my brother greeted as he swung around from a console and spread his arms wide. Wearing a turquoise and palm print shirt, the red beard long and flaming, he could be the real life manifestation of one of his video merman king characters, minus the tail. "Welcome to my aerie home. You don't know how long I've wanted to show you this, sis."

I stood staring at him, my brother, sitting in his wheelchair atop his tropical bastion, one hand tapping a drumroll on the chair arm. "Amazing." Which wasn't what I was thinking. "Captain Firebeard. Didn't you have a video character called that?"

His face split in an enormous grin as he whirred toward me, stopping inches away and making braking noises. "That was Captain Bartholomew, the merman king. I guess I am a kind of merman king now, aren't I?" he said, indicating his paralyzed legs.

"Guess you are." I noted how the irises of his blue eyes were dilated. I swallowed hard.

"That character must have been prophetic without me even realizing it." He kept tapping on his chair arm. "Either way, I'm the master of my universe."

"I can see that. Are you still making those animations?"

"No, I closed the company years ago but now I paint and design and conjure and invent and am happier than a man without legs could ever be, little sis. Couldn't ask for anything more—except my legs, of course. Otherwise, I have everything I ever wanted: a beautiful place to live, surrounded by great people, and art. It's all good."

So why did I have a tight little knot in my gut? "How can you afford all this?"

"What kind of question is that? You know I'm a rich man, Phoebe. Didn't I send you all that money a few years back?"

"Yes, you did. I thought it was from your animation company."

"And so it was."

I tried to smile. "I'm glad you're happy here but what about your freedom?"

"Freedom's all relative when you've lost your legs, Phoebe. This is my new freedom."

"But you're a hunted man, Toby."

He waved away the thought. "It doesn't feel that way where I'm sitting. I don't go anywhere, anyway, except maybe a few cruises on my boat. Besides, I can move—look." He performed a kind of whirling maneuver with his wheelchair. "See? All good. This is where I want to be. I'm not on the run, Phoebe, I'm on a roll." And he laughed at his own joke. "As for keeping away those who attempt to spoil my paradise, we are managing very well. Come, let me show you how it all works."

I followed him over to the console, which appeared to be a couple of flat-screened computers embedded into a vertical counter. There were other devices and controls, too, but I didn't grasp their significance. "See, we have cams all over the island so we can watch every-thing that's going on 24/7. There's always someone keeping watch, but this is my private tower. Very few people try arriving unannounced, anyway, I can tell you that."

"But people know you're here."

"Some do but those that matter think we're up to something else. We have loyal staff who are like our extended family. The locals working for us feel that they've died and gone to heaven they are treated so well. Captain Firebeard is a benevolent ruler. Everybody's got their own cottage and the wages are good."

"Somebody else said something similar to me not long ago," I whispered.

But Toby kept on talking. "We can see visitors coming from miles away and are always ready for them." He spun his chair again.

"You mean with guns and ammo?"

Toby chuckled and cast me a quick glance. "No, Phoebe. It doesn't pay to shoot up the government types. We start with a little greeting party—usually Lee and Barbara—who show any inspectors or officials around the island, explaining our resort plans. We even have blueprints written up with Peaches standing by to bury them with engineer-speak. And, of course, if somebody needs to be bought off to keep quiet, we do that, too. Our island paradise is slated to become the Captain Fire-beard Dreamscape Resort, or at least that's how we're priming it to appear."

I choked out a laugh. "Wow, it's like you've taken a page right out of Sir Rupert Fox's book, only with special effects."

"I never met Sir Foxy but Noel's told me all about him."

I tried to catch Max's eye but he was staring out at the sea, hands shoved into his pockets.

"And when the gangs and drug lords drop by?"

"Oh, those we shoot," my brother said with a shrug.

"Just like that," I said. "Bang bang." Suddenly, my legs were trembling.

"More like *kaboom*. Not all of them are on our hit list but most are. The cops turn a blind eye since we're helping rid the island of vermin —makes their jobs easier. Mostly the gangs leave us alone, except the

Willies, of course. Sorry you got snarled up with that lot, but we still managed to knock off four of them the night Noel rescued you from the reef. That ought to teach them that we mean business."

"Knock them off." Visions of his war-game videos flooded my memory. Though the scenes were fantastical, the object had always been to shoot as many of the enemy as possible with as much fire and video explosions as animation could contrive. His award-winning games were graphically powerful and as violent as hell. "Those were real humans you killed, even if Roger has a personal vendetta against you."

"Roger's a twisted piece of work. Can't get over the fact that his family likes me better than him. We used to get along all right once. Or at least we had a kind of working agreement." He paused, one finger on his chin, gazing out toward the sea.

Taking a step closer, I pulled over a stool before I toppled over. "How so?"

"You know, a you-scratch-my-back-and-I'll-scratch-yours kind of thing," he replied, whipping his chair around to face me. "You're asking a lot of questions there, little sis."

I took a deep breath, my hands gripping my knees. "We have a lot of stuff to catch up on, don't we, big bro?"

"Yes, we do, but maybe not all at once. You always were like that, you know," he said, smiling. "You always would ask piles of questions from your big bro and follow him around like a little puppy dog even when he tried to kick you away."

My turn to shrug, which hurt like hell. "I only followed you because you were my big brother and I worshipped you, and you never answered my questions—not fully, anyway—which only stoked my curiosity about where you went and what you were up to. Still does." I rubbed my shoulder.

"Yeah, some things never change. And every time you follow me, you get hurt or drag the enemy closer on my tail, just like before. You do see that, don't you? I love you, Phoebe, but you're a liability."

"A liability," I repeated. "Yes, I do see that. You didn't want me to come, did you?"

He shook his head so quickly it reminded me of a dog shaking water off its coat. "No. Noel and I fought about it. It's getting harder and harder for him to leave the island with all this renewed gang activity and so much Interpol attention. He still wants to go, though I need him to stay and take care of business. Besides, we have enough loot to keep us going for a while so he doesn't have to do any more jobs. But he needed to see you in person, he said. I figure maybe I should, too. Things went south just like I anticipated."

"Max and I came here because we wanted to. Remember, I'm not some sniveling kid anymore." Though I was close to sniveling right then.

"I'm sorry, Phoebe—sorry for all the pain I've caused you and all the harm I've put in your way but it's your fault."

"My fault?"

"You cause a shit-storm by following me. I love you but our lives have taken divergent paths. Nothing's going to change that. This has to be the last time we see one another, for your sake and mine. After this, you must pretend that you don't have a brother. Forget about me."

I stared at him. "How can I even do that? You're my only living relative, my *brother*."

"You must. Now that you can see how well we are living, maybe that will set your mind to rest. But tomorrow, you'll have to leave and never come back. You can understand why, don't you?"

"I think we can make that decision for ourselves, Toby," Max said, joining us at last.

Toby glanced up at him. "I know that you and Noel have your own matters to settle, and I'll leave that to you both, but I'm addressing my sister here, Max, so butt out." He turned back to me. "And you stay out of this mess, Phoebe. It's my mess, not yours. You've made it yours by chasing me around all over the world. Go away and never come back. Live your own life and let me live mine."

He leaned forward to take my hands, which was when I noticed the needle tracks on his arms. I snatched them away. "Does Noel feel the same way?"

"You'll have to ask him. Either way, this is our world now, Phoebe. It'll never be yours and you know it."

The lump in my throat hardened so much it became difficult to speak. "You're a user."

"Come again?"

"You're using drugs, aren't you? What is it...heroin, coke?"

He laughed. "Oh, little sis. Those are old hat. Anyway, a man has to ease his pain however he can. Don't you worry about it."

"But, Toby, you're killing yourself and there are gangs out there trying to kill you, too, plus you've been on Interpol's most-wanted list for years. This can't last. Surely you see that? It's only a matter of time before somebody breaks your defenses or your body collapses or, in the very best scenario, Interpol drags you off to prison."

"If anybody tries dragging me anywhere, I'll blow myself up and take this place with it, and should the enemy come anywhere near us, kaboom to them, too." He splayed his hands.

"Are you serious? This isn't one of your video games, Toby. This is real."

"Do I look like I'm playacting to you, sis?"

Sis. He never called me *sis* before. He called me Phoebe, his Phoebe.

I felt Max's hand land on my shoulder. "Come on, Phoebe. Let's get you back to your room for a rest, what do you say? This isn't going anywhere."

I took a deep breath and flung out one last question. "What about all the art and treasures you've absconded over the years?"

"What about them?" Toby asked, his face a mask.

I met my brother's eyes, the same shade of blue as mine, our shared DNA obvious in our coloring at least. "You're still trying to return those pieces to the countries of their origin, right?"

Something flickered deep in his gaze, something dark and inscrutable, something that chilled me to the bone. "What do you think?" I think Max is right and you do need to rest. I keep forgetting how much crap you've been through in the last few days, little sis. You go lay down, girl. We're having a celebratory dinner tonight so we want you fit for that, right?" And he gave me one of his big grins. "Let's enjoy our time together while we have it."

I got to my feet and stared down at him, afraid to speak for fear of breaking down. Moments later and I was heading down the elevator with Max.

"Toby's changed, too," I whispered. "He's not the same man I knew."

Max put his arm over my shoulders and pulled me close. "He's the same as always, darlin'. You just saw him through a little sister's eyes. He was your clever, talented big brother, a hero who could do no wrong. But I knew him differently. Even back in Nova Scotia, he was shifty and secretive. The idea to steal Alistair Wyndridge's treasures and replace them with forgeries was his, remember? He started this whole damn hell-ride."

❧ 18 ❧

Forget the wounded leg, the aching shoulder. Punched in the heart was my true affliction, everything else was mere surface noise.

My capacity for rationalization and self-delusion apparently knew no bounds. If I had allowed myself to imagine my brother beyond all evidence to the contrary, where did that leave Noel?

Love can make us do anything. Love can make us blind and stupid, stupid, stupid, but I had no one to blame but myself.

I had left Max at my bedroom door so I could grapple with the truth alone but remaining still when my heart was warred never worked for me. I had to move. Moments later, I was shuffling out the back door following the winding paths opposite the route taken the night before. I had no fixed direction, I just needed to move.

But solitude didn't come easily on the island. The grounds were hyperactive with people manicuring the lawns or dashing from cottage to cottage with cleaning wagons. A woman sweeping the paths of poinciana and frangipani petals greeted me in passing. "A fulljoy day, madam." She grinned.

I smiled. A fulljoy day. Well, I suppose it was a day full of joy if natural beauty, friendly faces, and luxury were the only necessary ingredients. If truth, honesty, integrity, and a purpose beyond oneself were also critical to one's happiness, then this was no paradise.

As I rounded a bend, a male peacock strutted across the lawn toward me, fixed me with its beady little eyes, and proceeded to unfurl his glory, brilliant feathers shimmering in the sun.

"Thank you." It would be churlish to walk by without comment. "But you realize we can't be mates, don't you?" I said aloud. "It doesn't matter how much we care for one another or how deep our attraction, we're two creatures living on opposite ends of the spectrum—too different, too far away from one another. It just can't be."

The peacock eyed me for a moment, closed his tail feathers, and sauntered off. Proper thing. At least some creatures knew when to move on. I squelched my overwhelming need to cry and carried along the path to the back of the house where doors had been thrown open to the breeze. I stepped into a dining room where two children, a boy and a girl, were filling glass vases with hibiscus flowers.

"Hi," I greeted as I stepped in.

They smiled shyly, their faces merry and sweet.

"Could you tell me where Mrs. Williams is?"

The little girl pointed to the door.

"Thanks."

I found Barbara in the kitchen directing operations with three others in the midst of a cooking storm. Cakes and buns, breads and pies, sat cooling on the counter, and whatever simmered on the stoves smelled divine. Spotting me, she sailed forward, her apron dusted in flour.

"Phoebe, are you hungry? We have food here to feed a nation, Lord knows we do. Your brother is feeding the staff, too, and they will have their own party on the lawn. Meet our chefs. Jerome, you got a minute?"

Jerome, wearing a white chef's hat and chopping vegetables, the only male in the team, lifted his head and waved. "Hi, Phoebe. You be enjoyin' our island?"

"Sure thing," I said, returning his grin. "Well, I'll just let you all get back to work." I didn't feel like smalltalk.

I don't know what I was hoping for in tracking down Barbara—

JANE THORNLEY

someone to talk to, I guess. I'd sent Max away saying that I needed to think, which was true, but I also needed to talk, but only to someone who lived here. Everyone seemed too busy for real conversation. Maybe the answers I wanted wouldn't come easily, anyway.

I slipped away from the kitchen, passing through rooms filled with flowers, a fully stocked bar, another pool, and more patios. When I reached the elevator to Toby's lighthouse, I stepped inside and studied the buttons—four levels with the fourth floor being the topmost. I pressed down instead of up. I had no idea where I was going.

The doors swished open to what I presumed to be the basement level. Ahead, a woman could be seen making a bed in a room beyond. I removed my flip-flops and silently skirted the bedroom to dart into the suite of rooms beyond.

One glance registered the wheelchair-accessible furnishings, the low tables, the relatively wide spaces. This had to be Toby's private quarters. I was just about to slip out when my gaze flew to the walls and I almost gasped. What the floor lacked in furnishings, the walls compensated in art. Gold objects gleamed in glass cabinets—mostly Spanish and Aztec pieces—but there were other artifacts dating from the Greek and Roman periods, too, plus an impressive number of paintings—sober Renaissance pieces, a few eighteenth century portraits, a few Impressionist works. Most were encased in tempera-ture and humidity-controlled glass. Though not recognizable by me, I knew they were probably priceless. And original. And none of them should be here, not one.

Numb, I wandered around, seeing but not seeing, struggling with disbelief. My brother had amassed a sizable collection reminiscent of Roger Williams's but more carefully curated. My brother was a collector of a similar ilk to Rupert; only, in his case, it had all been stolen. *Stolen.* This is what had become of all the antiquities they had robbed from the greedy to give to the common good? The irony killed me.

The sound of a wheeled bucket rolling around a tiled floor next door sent me scrambling for the elevator. As I pushed the button, I caught a glimpse of the woman about to tackle a bathroom with a mop. Our eyes locked as the door swept shut. She called out to me but I kept on going, my heart beating a crazy dance in my chest.

The elevator took me to the third floor. I knew I really should leave, that I'd already seen more than enough, but as long as there was one more floor, that had to be my destination.

The scent of paint and linseed oil reached me before the door even opened. When I stepped into another wide window-surround space and gazed at the easels propped there, I recognized it as Toby's studio. My brother the artist, my brother the creative genius. Hadn't I always thought of him that way, considered him far above the rest of mere mortals by virtue of his amazing talent?

I stepped forward. Three easels stood side by side, each of them bearing exactly the same portrait in various stages of completion, that of a long-haired young man gazing at the viewer, a velvet cap worn far back on his head, a fur mantle over his shoulders—Raphael as a young man. Only one painting had been completed and though it looked authentically Renaissance to the untrained eye, the paint was still wet. So where was the original?

"Lady, you should not be here now."

I swung around. The maid stood at the elevator door. "This be the Captain's quarters and he do not like people here."

"I'm his sister," I said, not quite stripping the emotion from my voice. "I just wanted to see where he lived."

She smiled. "Welcome to the island but you be leaving now. Nobody allowed in here. You ask and he show you."

I nodded. "Sorry." I shuffled out, snatching up my flip-flops and escaping.

I was a lawyer by training, had been schooled in rational thinking as well as the artistic and retail life of my recent experience. Some of my approaches to gathering evidence might be likened to any detective, any lawyer, but what happens when reason rams into the heart, Sherlock? Oh, wait, Sherlock Holmes was all deduction. His heart had been amputated by his intellect, presumably. Mine was just a mess.

Maybe I needed more information, even a confession of sorts, before reaching any hideous conclusion? But I was only fooling myself. I already knew the truth.

Again, I didn't care where I was going. At the top of the ramp, I hung a right, pushing through the screen door into a shady glade. Paths crisscrossed in all directions and, in the style of any well-tended tropical retreat, little signs were posted pointing to various locations. I took the one marked *Beach*.

As the path narrowed, the jungle rose up overhead and sun filtered through the branches in long motes that caught the flash of bird and butterfly wing. I broke through the foliage to a small sheltered beach where a ridge of flotsam and tide leavings grimed the sandy crescent. An islet shone in the sun across the cove not more than a hundred yards away, the top of a turret gleaming through the palms. Peaches's bridge leaped the narrows further along the shore.

I slipped from my flip-flops and dropped my robe onto a rock, watching it pool into a silky puddle on the sand as I stepped into the water. In seconds I was paddling toward the islet, hoping that my actions would remain unseen from the hundreds of eyes that must monitor this island. The water stroked my skin, every part of my being reveling in the warm ocean despite the stings, despite the lead weight of my heart that should by rights drag me to the bottom.

As far as I knew, I made it across the channel without attracting notice. At last, I hauled myself to shore and plunged through the jungle without prompting a call or cry of alarm. The island was mostly natural jungle with no effort made to tame the wild tangles that grew there so I proceeded carefully, picking through vines as soundlessly as I could manage.

The tower folly rearing through the palms was my only destination. As I grew closer, I saw that the stucco exterior was covered in fading paint, an art nouveau floral design barely visible on its weathered surface. Maybe fifty feet tall, the structure appeared old enough to be original to Heston Finn's time and obviously not part of the renovations that had transformed the rest of Toby's buildings, at least not externally. There was the matter of that low whining hum emanating from within.

Slowly, I followed the building's circumference until I could see a path darting down a hill toward the shore. The figure of a tall man could just be seen standing with his back toward me. A stab of fear mixed with a thousand other emotions hit my gut but I still continued until I stood at the door with its keypad entrance. I pushed at the door but it didn't budge. I expected that. I also expected that my attempts to gain entrance by pounding on the steel surface would eventually catch the attention of the guard.

"Phoebe, what the hell are you doing here?"

I turned. "What does it look like, Noel?"

His face flashed with conflicting emotions, most of them probably mirrored by mine—anger, love (was I only imagining that?), fear, and something else that forced his gaze away. "This island is off-limits for a reason."

I snorted. "Let me guess: because it's a climate-controlled vault for priceless antiquities—that is, whatever items you two have decided not to keep for yourselves?"

"I kept nothing for myself, let me make that perfectly clear." Anger strung his voice. "But, Phoebe," he said, his tone softening as he stepped toward me. "I needed you to come here and see what's happening for yourself. There was no other way I could tell you every-thing you needed to know, but I didn't factor on the hurricane or you getting kidnapped by Roger Williams. Bringing you here was a mistake. It was too dangerous, too hurtful, but I needed to see you one more time. I couldn't bear to imagine you never knowing, always wondering."

"Never knowing that my brother and my lover are thieves, plain and simple, with nothing the least bit noble about a damn thing they've done? Is that what you wanted me to see for myself?"

"It's not that simple. I—"

"It's simple enough. Everything else is just window-dressing. Is that why you've been avoiding me?"

"Partly," he said softly, "but, Phoebe, believe me, there's much more I have to tell you."

"Skip the tender words—that is, if you were planning any. Toby has informed me that after tonight's family reunion—God, don't let me choke on that word—I'm to leave this island and never see either of you again. I'm a liability, I get it. Are you in on this?"

"I swear I didn't want any of this to happen, Phoebe, but it has to be this way, surely you can see that? After tonight, I agree with Toby that we can have no more contact, for all our sakes." His gaze caressed my face before swerving away to focus on some undetermined spot overhead.

My eyes followed his and I saw the camera positioned under the turret roof but that didn't stop me. "Look at me!" He returned his gaze to mine but the pain I witnessed there was almost too raw to look at. "I mean, are you in on this travesty of stealing priceless art and antiquities and keeping them instead of repatriating them like you led me to believe? I want to hear you say it."

"I—my intentions were honorable in the beginning, I swear, but the situation changed. That's all I can say."

"That's enough!" I pushed past him, heading for the bridge.

"Phoebe, wait!"

I turned.

"Nothing changes how I feel about you, believe that, absolutely nothing!" he called after me.

"But it changes how I feel about you," I told him.

But that was a lie. I'd always love that man no matter what he did.

❧ 19 ❧

My prescription for pain has always been to knit. Failing that, I hand-wind yarn. Failing that, I wash said yarn, letting the strands caress my fingers. It's a tactile thing. Yarn to me is a hug waiting to happen and right then I needed to self-medicate any way I could. Real drugs were never an option.

I spent the rest of the day cloistered in my room, deconstructing my unborn wrap, first removing the river-grimed stitches from the needles and then washing the fibers in the sink with coconut shampoo. I did likewise with each of the balls I'd brought, hanging them up to dry in the sun afterward, their colors streaming in the breeze like little flags of hope.

One visitor after the other came to see me that afternoon. First Lee arrived to change my bandage, though I was perfectly able to administer to my wound myself. Once he'd finished, he hung around as if wanting to say something. I made it easy for him. "I know my brother is a drug addict, Lee. Is that what you wanted to tell me?"

He looked startled but rallied quickly. "Oh, dear Phoebe, I am most sorry but yes, I'm afraid that is true. When I first came here to tend Noel years ago, I discovered Tobias to be in constant pain. The bullet wound he suffered has created irrevocable damage to his spine, and there is little one can do to help such cases but attempt to ease the agony."

"So you prescribed something."

"Oxycodin at first. I thought that a spate of three days only would grant him some brief respite while we embarked on a series of pain management videos. That was a mistake. He would not accept temporary relief. Once he experienced the drugs, there was no going back."

"My brother never accepts half of anything. It has to be all or nothing." There was bitterness in my voice and I didn't care.

"I should have known better, truly. Meanwhile, unbeknownst to me, he had already contacted my son and begun purchasing stronger, more addictive substances."

"While paying for them with the antiquities he amassed. Peaches told me and I figured out the rest." My voice sounded too calm, even to me—numb, almost. I suppose I was locked down into survival mode.

"Eventually, yes, but I did not ask those questions. I only begged him to stop but he would not. He claims nothing else alleviates his agony. Now I fear it is too late." He lifted his hands and let them drop.

"Because he's an addict."

"In the early stages, but yes, and I hold myself responsible."

I touched his arm, my emotions thawing at last. "Lee, my brother made his own decision to strike up business with your son. That's on him. So is his paralysis. He was shot while stealing a fortune of artifacts from a man he tricked into loving him. You are not responsible."

He studied me intently. "Phoebe, you do not make your brother sound like a good person."

"He isn't, and believe me, it's taken me a long time and many traumas to reach that conclusion. In fact, I've only just arrived."

He rubbed his eyes. "And yet, here we are."

"And yet, here we are. My brother is as much a criminal as your son, only maybe less brutal, but who knows what the drugs will make him descend into? You have to save yourselves while you still can."

"I cannot leave here, Phoebe, not as long as my own son lives across the way as his murderous self."

"If you can't save your son or my brother, save yourselves. Save what matters. Do what's in your control. Take your family and leave this island while you still can."

"And do what, Phoebe?" I swung around to see Barbara standing at the entranceway. She entered quickly, shutting the door behind her. "This is our home now and here we stay. Besides, we can no more leave Tobias than we can Roger. They are both part of our troubled family now. Lord knows but we are caught between them both."

She came within inches of me. "It's Peaches who must leave but we cannot convince her to go. You must help."

"Me?" I asked.

"You, child. Tomorrow morning Tobias has arranged a boat to take you and Max to Montego Bay for a flight back to London. Peaches must go with you, but as a stowaway."

"Tobias cannot know," Lee hastened to add. "He refuses to let her go."

"What?" I asked, turning to him. "Are you saying that Toby has Peaches held in some kind of indentured servitude?"

"In a manner of speaking, yes," Barbara said. "Everyone who works for him is, to one extent or another, his. For Lee and me it doesn't matter because here we will stay, want to stay, *must* stay. Your brother even turned the deed of the island over to us—for his own protection, but nevertheless. In return, we help Tobias and keep things steady for those who live and work here—those who want to remain, which be most of them. And as long as we are here, Roger will not launch a full attack. We are Tobias's insurance. It is our Peaches who needs to break free."

I began pacing the room. "What about Noel, where does he fit into all this?" When they didn't respond immediately, I searched their faces, one after the other. "What?"

"We do not know, Phoebe," Lee began. "Noel has kept his own counsel for some time now. I believe something is afoot but I have no idea what."

"They argue a great deal, those two," Barbara said with a nod. "My thinking is that Noel is not happy about the recent turn of events."

"No, of course not. How could he be?" I said. "They used to be friends those two, equals in their noble plan to return the world's art heritage to the hands of the people." I almost choked on the words. All the pieces were beginning to fit. "Besides you two and Peaches and Max, who else here can I trust?" I could not afford to add Noel to that list, I knew that much.

"No one," Lee said. "All the staff remains loyal to Captain Firebeard. We will help you smuggle Peaches away but only in secret."

I nodded. "Let me think on how we're going to do this and we'll talk more later."

But before they left, Peaches arrived. "Hi, Mom, Dad, Phoebe. Has the meeting started without me?"

"I take it this is no coincidence," I asked her as she stepped into my now-crowded room.

"No, not a coincidence, I was told to come."

"We asked you to meet us here, Penelope," her mother said with exaggerated patience.

"Yes, and I live to serve, but, Phoebe, look what I found on de beach." She held up my flip-flops and sodden robe. "Dis ting was soaked and de flowered flops were floating on de tide. Did you just leave dem dere?"

"Speak proper English, girl," her mother admonished as I whipped the crumpled ball from her hands and tossed it into the bathroom sink.

"So, you all talking about me?" I heard Peaches ask.

"Your name came up," her mother answered.

"Yes, it did," I said, stepping back into the room. "Right after we discussed how my brother, the art thief, is also a drug addict, and how I now realize he's been hoarding all the antiquities he's stolen to feed his lifestyle. This has been a day of revelations for me."

Peaches whistled between her teeth. "You okay with dis shit, Phoebe?"

"Penelope Susanne Marie, watch your mouth!" her mother ordered.

"I am not all right with this shit, that's the point," I said, holding Peaches's gaze with my own. "I am definitely not all right with any of it. I thought my brother and Noel were repatriating these pieces to public repositories when the whole damn time they were gilding their own nest."

She held up her hands. "So, your brother is almost as bad as mine only much more fun. De Captain's been selling tings to the Willies to finance this whole operation, but look, compared to my brother, yours is still a saint. I told you dey were sinking, Phoebe. The whole friggin' ting is coming undone. Wish I could build a bridge to prop dem all up but I can't."

"Penelope, speak the Queen's English, not Jamaican-speak," her father admonished.

"Stop it, Papa! Stop it both of you!" Peaches cried. "I belong to Jamaica, not the queen, and proud of it. I'm just not proud of becoming whatever the hell it is I am now. Let me talk how I feel."

"Hush, daughter mine," Lee said, taking his daughter in his arms. "Lower your voice. This island has ears." As he patted her back, she struggled for a moment but then settled into his embrace and continued in a half whisper. "Now listen, my child. Tomorrow the Captain is sending Phoebe and Max from the island. You must go with them."

"Me, why?" Peaches pulled away. She stood at least a foot taller than him and soared way over her mother.

"Because we need you safe," Barbara replied. "We need you off the island and living your life, not hanging on here because of us."

"I can't just leave you!" Peaches said, her voice rising again.

Her mother put a finger to her lips. "Yes, you can. You must. Tomorrow you must go with Phoebe. We will find a way."

"I will find a way," I said firmly. "I already have the beginnings of a plan."

Peaches turned to me, her gaze steady and unflinching. "You?"

"Yes, me. You don't know what I'm capable of." Half the time, neither did I. "Trust me."

"Trust don't come easily these days."

"*Doesn't* or *does not*," Barbara corrected. "Not *don't*."

"Ma used to be a teacher. Can't you tell?" Peaches said to me before turning to her mother and adding: "Cut it out, Ma. I'm all emotional right now so my elocution just doesn't feature." Peaches began to pace the room, her long legs making the circumference at twice my speed. We almost collided.

I stopped, turning to Barbara and Lee. "How about letting Peaches and me talk alone?"

Barbara placed her hand on her husband's arm. "Yes, indeed. We've got work to do preparing for tonight's event, anyway. We must ensure the fireworks are set up and the band is ready to play. Toby means to make this quite a night, I can tell you. We shall talk later."

Lee nodded and the two of them left, though that didn't stop Peaches from striding around the room.

"Yeah, right, so it wasn't always like dis," she said on her circular pace. "When I first came here, I really tot I was to be dere engineer. Like, I'm not an architect but I know de basics. I can draw up a blueprint so I helped dem draw up de plans and I designed de bridge. I had ideas, dey had ideas—or he did, your brother. It was wild, like I tot I'd died and gone to heaven—great bosses, money, the job I love."

"And Noel?"

She stopped and stared at me. "I never had anyting going on with him and not because I didn't try."

"I don't mean romantically. I mean, what did he say about the things Toby was getting up to?"

"Your hottie never had much to say 'bout anyting, but I never tot he was happy. I didn't ask where de the money was coming from until de Captain, he asked me to work a deal with my brother. Dat was de start. Dat was when de rot set in."

"And then my brother became an addict."

"He was already on de way. Lots of addicts where de money flows and de people don't recognize despair. I felt sorry for him but den he got dangerous."

"But letting things go on this way will only make it worse. Toby and Noel can't keep this going, not with your brother bearing down and Interpol hot on their tails. It's all going to end, and when it does, it won't be pretty. They're going to die, Peaches. Somebody is going to kill them. We have to set things straight before that happens."

"Whoa!" Peaches held up her hands. "How are we going to set tings straight?"

"Trust me, that's all I ask. I have an idea that will protect your folks and everyone on this island while dealing with a crime that has to stop.

You said you wanted to do good in the world so let's start with what's here. Let's take the plunge. Are you with me?"

Her eyes narrowed. "What have you got planned?"

"As soon as I pull the pieces together, I'll let you know, but it involves a change, a really big one. I'll need the blueprints of the island you drew up and anything you may have about that folly."

"Folly?"

"The little tower vault Toby has on the mini island."

"Right, the vault."

"Do you know what's in there?"

"Never seen inside since I designed the ting."

"I believe stolen art is being stored in there. If you designed it, you can probably figure out a way to get inside without damaging anything. That's important. So, can you get those blueprints for me?"

"I'll tink about it," she said on her way out the door. "Are you planning to steal whatever's in there, is dat it? If you do, you'll be as bad as de Captain and he'll pull every trick in the book to protect dat loot."

"Whatever's in that vault has no business being there. It needs to go back to where it belongs and not be used as barter for drugs. Still working on the specifics."

"Can't commit without de details, no matter what my folks say. I'll be back."

No sooner had she left than I was pulling the Vuitton roller from the closet. The garbage bag had offered protection against the elements, thus preserving my designer wardrobe, but I was more interested in what else Nicolina had packed.

Feeling along the bottom of the case, I released the catch and lifted out the false bottom followed by the sheet of anti-X-ray deflector Evan had devised. I stared. Nicolina had packed a smartphone along with the tin of detector mints she had mentioned. I smiled. It's good to have friends who knew what you needed before you did.

As the phone powered up, I flipped the tin lid. There really were mints in there, pretty little pink things that wafted menthol, and yet apparently I was now sending my coordinates to Nicolina.

After that, I felt inside of the lining of my still-damp carpetbag, finding a fold of paper along with the business card Nicolina had given me. I stared at Noel's paper, still crisp and jotted with little inscrutable symbols. Noel, oh, hell, Noel! But I had to focus and study that code some other time. For now I focused on the business card—still legible but barely. In seconds, I was phoning Montego Bay and asking to speak to Lucas Brown.

"Lucas at your service, concierge at the Washing Sands Resort. I put the *don't worry* and *be happy* into your every day."

"Lucas? Phoebe McCabe here. Nicolina Vanvitelli gave me your contact number and said you'd help me."

There was a pause. "Yes, Phoebe. I've been tinking you might call. How can I help you?"

"Ah." I gazed out toward the patio where my peacock suitor had arrived, presumably to ask for a second chance. "We're renovating a resort here and have run out of supplies. I was hoping you could help us locate the necessary items."

"Certainly. What do you need and when do you need them?"

"Could I send you a list?"

When Max came by an hour later, my yarn was drying, my robe was hanging up in the breeze, and I had just managed to lay one hundred slightly damp stitches on my needles as I sat perched on the edge of the bed. Beside me on a wad of paper, I had jotted down lines of knit code—k1, k2tog, and so on—using my own special abbreviations to align with Noel's symbols. It was pretty rough even for me but I could polish up the details later.

"Back in therapy, I see," he said as he stepped through the door.

I looked up at my godfather and caught the strain in his face beneath the sunburn. "Yes, and feeling much better for it. For one thing, I finally have my resolution in line along with my stitches. Would you like to hear what I've decided?"

He raked one hand through his shower-slicked hair. "I do, Phoebe, my girl. Feel up to a little stroll under the trees while we talk?"

I set my knitting aside and stood up. "Sure."

Linking my arm in his, we stepped out through the patio doors and across the lawn. "Before I begin," I said, "I just want you to understand that my decisions are mine alone. It's not that I don't care how they affect you because I do—deeply—but I need to take the initiative and not wait for others to set things straight. Make sense so far?"

"Yes, Phoebe, it does." He squeezed my arm.

"And I don't want to influence you one way or the other regarding the fallout. Whatever you decide, I promise to accept it no matter what."

"Why don't you just spit it out, darlin'?"

❧ 20 ❧

I had never truly understood the meaning of a broken heart until that moment. That a heart could sustain multiple fractures and still keep beating *and loving* was news to me. It is possible to still function while struggling with guilt and pain and to do so in the spirit of love, though a younger self would never have understood. And, even more importantly, it is possible to act based on that love, regardless of the consequences.

Maybe that's called growing up, the kind of emotional growth that has nothing to do with chronological years. Staring at myself in the mirror that evening, I could even see the changes in my face. The eyes gave it away. The anger had drained and something deeper and more resolute had taken hold.

Externally, I looked amazing. When a woman is about to say goodbye to the man she loves, she needs the right clothes. Call it emotional self-defense, call it insecurity, call it whatever you want, but that night I was grateful for my designer wardrobe if for no other reason than it removed me from myself.

I chose the hydrangea silk skirt and off-shoulder blouse and combed my hair the way the Dolce & Gabanna women had shown me. In an added flourish, I picked a peachy-toned hibiscus from outside and tucked it behind my ear. Staring in the mirror, I was almost unrecognizable, at least to myself. If it weren't for the bruise on my temple and the steely grit touched with sadness in my eyes, I might be some lovely heroine ensorcelled on a magic island about to meet her fairy lover.

Night had fallen deep and velvety-lush across the island when I stepped out the patio door and followed the path toward the entrance of the main house. Don't ask me why I didn't just take the interior route to the dining room. I guess I needed a grand entrance, as if I'd drifted into the gathering caught on a passing trade wind and could just as easily drift away. In truth, my planned escape would be more turbo-boosted.

The steely pulse of a calypso band was playing away on the other side of the island when I stepped across the threshold into the candlelit house. I followed the sound of voices into the lounge where Toby was entertaining his audience with some story or other while Lee and Barbara stood by, laughing with drinks in their hands. Peaches and Max hung back, quietly watching, but lifted their glasses to me when I appeared. At first I didn't see Noel.

A man dressed in green tights and a sparkly tunic slid up to me, bowed, and extended a tray of champagne flutes. I took one, lifted my glass to Max and Peaches, and caught Max's nod. Peaches was gleaming in some kind of tight silver sheath that made her look simultaneously gorgeous and lethal. I toasted them both.

"Phoebe," I heard a voice softly say behind me.

I turned. Noel stood watching me from the shadows, all dark-eyed and intense, his black hair damp and curling around the collar of his white shirt. My heart thumped crazily as he stepped away from the wall to stand close to me, gazing down. I inhaled the scent of shampoo and soap and...

"What is that spicy cologne you use? I always meant to ask."

He smiled. "Bay Rum, and it's not cologne but aftershave. A manly man doesn't wear cologne."

"Oh, of course. How could I think otherwise?" But despite the lilt of bonhomie, the emotions streaming between us were anything but light. I could not take my eyes off him. For precious seconds we held one another's gaze, caught in our own private world. If I could hold that moment safe forevermore, I would. I'd let nothing destroy it, nothing damage that hold, but it wasn't to be.

"Phoebe, you look beautiful tonight, but then, to me you always are."

"Noel, I didn't mean what I said earlier."

"I know, but I don't blame you for reacting the way you did. Phoebe, I need to tell you—"

"There you are, little sis!" Toby boomed from across the room. "Come join us, you two! Dinner's waiting and it's party time!"

I swung around and tried to smile. "Toby," I said.

"Come on down!" my brother bellowed. "Chow's on."

Noel and I followed Toby's chair across the polished tiles into the flower-strewn dining room, the rest of the group trailing in behind. We had assigned seating, every place marked by a card with one of my brother's video characters sketched in marker pen with our names scrolled in his bold script. Mine came with a big-breasted mermaid complete with a fetching lime-green tail and Toby's was a king-sized male version with turquoise fins, a crown, and a trident. Mer-people had been our childhood emblems, though thirty years ago ours had been more or less of equal size.

Toby claimed the head of the table with me to his right, Max across from me, and Noel beside him opposite Peaches. Lee was sitting at the other end facing my brother with Barbara on his right-hand side. Though Noel attempted to switch places with Peaches to my left, Toby waved him away. We were to sit where we were told, no options entertained. Peaches caught my eye and grimaced.

Folding my hands in my lap, I waited as candlelight flickered across the gathering. The only ones who appeared to indulge Toby's fantasy were Lee and Barbara, who seemed to be playing courtiers to his royal persona. Barbara, dressed in a long green gown, swept up to his seat carrying a crown on a blue velvet pillow. "For you, Captain Firebeard," she said with a curtsy. I watched dumbstruck as Toby lifted the gleaming gold and jeweled piece from its bed and placed it on his head.

"That looks real," I said.

"Margaret of York, one of only two such pieces in the world. What do you think?" my brother asked, lifting is chin. "It's a bit small but a crown's a crown."

"Where did you get that?"

Toby grinned. "Had it for quite a while."

"Did you steal it or did Noel?" Max asked across from me.

"Does it matter?" Toby asked. "And enough with the questions! Let's make this night special since it will be our last together." He clapped his hands and three men dressed in bright green hose and tunics stepped in bearing silver platters of warm bread and trays of wine goblets.

"You're taking the indentured servitude thing a bit far, aren't you?" I asked.

"They enjoy the fun, why don't you, little sis? Don't be such a pain in the neck. It gets old really fast." He was twitching and a rim of sweat glossed his brow.

I caught Noel's gaze down the table and fell silent. This was all playacting, I realized, an extension of Toby's creative world, but it also communicated just how out of touch with reality my brother had become.

"So, little sis, you look mighty fetching tonight," Toby said to me. "I've never seen you decked out in so much finery. I can see you're using my largess to your best advantage," he said, fingers tapping away on his chair arm.

Okay, so I didn't stay silent long. "Pardon me? I didn't use the money you sent without my knowledge into my bank account to buy finery, brother mine. I used it to first find you, and then to alleviate some of the damage your actions caused while you continued stealing and forging art. And—"

He lifted his hands. "Whoa! I said let this be a fun night, so stop with the criticism. This is all for you, so try to have a little fun for once. Remember those dreamscapes I used to paint you?"

I did—brilliant, playful, bouncing with color and magic characters. "Yes, but that was—" Peaches kicked me under the table. "Fantastic."

What was the point of trying to counter his beleaguered thoughts? Play along, play along.

Though I sipped the champagne, I soon switched to water when the first platters of food arrived. My appetite had improved significantly so I dug into the curries and conch soup, the bowls of vegetables, and the rice dishes. Partly I was trying to distract myself from what was about to unfold, but mostly I was simply ravenous.

And there was Noel sitting at the end of the table with those fine lips twisted into distain at the pantomime going on around him. Nobody who knew that man could ever think he was happy—that is, until his gaze caught mine and he smiled. That moment became our moment, a blaze of hot joy I could never describe to anyone who had yet to experience it. Love, it can save us or kill us, sometimes both simultaneously. I could only pray that he'd forgive me the way I was trying to forgive him.

I wrenched my gaze away to check the time—10:15. It was all about to start. Beyond the wide-open doors, the steel band was either growing louder or closer, I couldn't tell, as the last of the dessert dishes were cleared away and the lights dimmed. I was so distracted it didn't matter. So much had to work perfectly that night and yet it had suddenly occurred to me how many things could go wrong. Everything, in fact.

Suddenly Toby raised his hands and shouted: "The entertainment has arrived! Enjoy yourselves, my friends!"

At last. As planned, Peaches shoved back her seat and stood up. "Max, get your butt up outta that chair and dance wit me!" she called. It was like a call to action. As she began hip-pulsing toward Max, who now stood up, Noel slipped behind me and offered his hand. "May I have this dance?"

That wasn't in the script, but then, he wasn't part of the cast, either. But why not? I had at least half an hour to enjoy the moment. "Sure," I said, putting my hand in his.

"Enjoy yourselves, kiddies," Toby called out as Noel tugged me out onto the torch-lit patio as fireworks popped silver plumes overhead.

"Oh, pretty!" I cooed.

"That's fireworks number one," Noel said as he swung me about in some kind of frantic waltz to the rhythm of the steel band that was now rumba-ing up the path. The band encircled us in a giant stream of gyrating movement, waving and calling out as they passed, as the rest of us either clapped our hands or danced.

"Ya, mon," the lead singer called out, raising a fist to Noel. "We dance for de king Firebeard and de guests!"

"Yeah!" Noel called out. "Dance for the king!"

At that, the troop, brilliant in yellow, green, and black skirts and trousers, broke into energetic pulsating movement, kicking their legs in the air, swaying around the patio and into the dining room in a huge living circle. Noel just kept twirling me around until I was forced to lean into him to steady myself.

"I'm getting dizzy," I whispered.

He held me tight and whispered back. "Just hang on to me. The music is about to slow way down."

Right on cue, the tempo smoothed into a sultry samba accompanied by a trio of singers crooning a refrain. I melted against him as he held me tight.

"Let de moon cry mi heart out, let de sea wash away de pain
  "For once I leave dis island, I will never be de same."

"I believe it," I said, resting my head on his shoulder. "We will never be the same after tonight."

My feet moved on their own volition, my heart throbbing with the beat. I could have stayed in his arms forever but some inner warrior reminded me that all was not well in paradise. Stumbling, I broke our rhythm and tried leading him gently back toward the dining room.

"Mi heart is a-breaking, mi feet move with de beat
  "But when I'm wit you, I only feel de heat."

"Stop that, Phoebe," he said, gazing down at me, the

intensity in his eyes belying the tiny smile. "The man is always in charge on the dance floor."

"As in life, so in dance? Maybe it's time that stopped. I've been following you and Toby for years and where has it gotten either me or you two—violence, terror, pending disaster? Maybe it's time for the woman to step up."

Noel gripped me by the waist and grinned. "And don't I just love a woman who steps up. Just not now."

"What's wrong with now?"

He pulled back. "Just let me do the manly thing for a few minutes longer. I have a plan in motion." He was now steering us off the patio and under the trees.

"But, Noel—"

"Just keep moving, Phoebe."

So I kept moving as he twirled me further and further away from the house. "What plan?" I asked, a little breathless from the music, the starlight, my proximity to the man.

"The band will keep Toby distracted awhile longer, hopefully long enough, and then the grand event kicks into motion—three small fireworks followed by one finale starburst, that last one being my signal." He took my hand and led me deeper under the trees.

"Signal for what?" I tugged him to a stop. "I have signals of my own. You tell me yours and I'll tell you mine."

We were deep in the foliage by now, the torch lights flickering like fireflies through the leaves. I could not see his face.

"OH, MI SUGAR SWEET, THE TIME IT HAS COME,
"Let dis kiss be our last but now you give me some."

"I'M GETTING OFF THIS ISLAND, PHOEBE, LEAVING THIS LIFE FOR good. That's why I had to bring you to Jamaica. I needed you to see Toby for yourself so you'd understand. I needed to talk to you in person before it all goes to hell. But nothing I do tonight changes my feelings for you ever, believe that."

My heart lurched. "Wait a minute. All these years I've done everything I can to keep you safe, no matter what the cost. I've kept your secrets and followed you halfway around the world twice over, always thinking the men I cared about were doing wrong things for the right reasons. Now I discover that you haven't been repatriating this art to their rightful homes at all. You're just common thieves and this has all been a sham!"

He stepped toward me. "It wasn't a sham, Phoebe. I started this endeavor with the best of intentions but my partners had other ideas. First Maggie and now Toby started keeping key pieces. At first I fought constantly trying to get the items back to their rightful owners but now I'm done, understand? Done. You see Captain Firebeard back there?" He pointed back toward the house. "That's what I've been living with for the past two years—drug-addled madness. I'm done trying to help that addict back there."

I took a step toward him. "So you're leaving, I got that, but where will you go?"

"Just away. I've got to break free from this prison, away from this life. No more stealing, no more trying to make a wrong act right. I've had enough."

A little bolt of joy hit. "Oh, wow, good." I reached for his hand and pulled him out into the open so I could see his face. "Does that mean you'll give yourself up?" I held his gaze with mine. "Look, I know how you hate the idea, but if you turn yourself in, I can work toward negotiating a lighter sentence. I have powerful lawyer friends back home, not to mention a connection with Interpol. All it takes is for you to release the treasures back to the authorities and turn yourselves in."

"Never." He pulled his hand away, leaving mine hanging in the empty air.

"Never? What do you mean by never? Noel, brutal bastards are trying to kill you both, and they'll succeed someday soon—if not the Willies, then somebody else. You shot a Camorra in Italy and a couple of Willies on the reef, remember? And those are only the ones I know about. You're on everybody's hit list. They'll kill you. It has to stop."

"It is stopping," he said, taking me by the shoulders. "It will stop tonight, but on my terms. Phoebe, think: how in hell do you think I'd survive prison, even for a short time?" He gave me a little shake. "With my enemies, I'd probably be executed within days. Crime doesn't stop at the prison door, no matter what you think. No, I'm going deep into hiding. I intend to drop off the face of the earth for however long it takes. I just needed to see you again before I left."

"But—"

And then he kissed me hard and once again my brain cells struggled to hang on to a single clear thought. I melted against him for the beat of seconds until the next fireworks bursting overhead startled me enough to push away. "Go where?" I cried. We were now standing washed in the stark silver light as the last fire-burst trails petered away.

"I can't tell you that, not for your sake nor mine," he said. "Someday I'll come back for you—that is, if you still want me, and some lucky bugger hasn't stepped in. I'm releasing you from whatever hold I've had on you, Phoebe. Find somebody worthy of you. Forget about me."

"If one more man tells me to forget about him, I'll kick him in the nuts. Look, Noel, you can't release me because we've never had the chance to be together in the first place, get it? I'm a free agent, you're a free agent." And all this free agent crap was bringing me to tears.

He smiled, one of those half-lip quirks that shot tremors through me. "And how sad is that? I find the love of my life and I can't have her. You know I want a life with you more than anything but I'm sure as hell not going to get it living like this. Maybe someday it will be different but not now."

"But we could negotiate a shorter prison term for you—maybe no more than a couple of years—and then you'll be free and we can be together."

"Did you hear a single thing I said? They'd kill me in there!"

"No, they wouldn't. There must be ways to set up protection, right? Put you in a special cell or something?" I sobbed.

"Stop it, Phoebe. I'm sure as hell not going to prison!"

"What about Toby? He's in desperate shape and he'd never go away with you, even if he could. He's killing himself. We have to save him."

"Save him how?" He stepped away, raking a hand through his hair. "You don't save addicts. They have to want to save themselves and

Toby doesn't, believe me. I've tried, God knows I've tried, but now I'm resigned to the fact that he's willing to die in his Captain Firebeard dreamworld while all the people around him go down with the ship. I've told Barb and Lee and the rest to get out, even offered them an exit plan, but they're not budging."

Another starburst exploded overhead, this one neon pink and accompanied by whistling noises. We both looked up. "That's number three," he said. "The next will be the big one."

But I was too focused on our conversation. "They won't leave him the way he is now. He's crazy, I know, but that makes him as vulnerable as hell. He needs to be forced into detox. He won't like it—in fact, he'll hate it and me, too, probably—but it's the only way, the only way to stop the violence."

"Maybe so, but that's not my battle. I've tried long enough. Let him go, Phoebe. I know you love him and it hurts like hell, but go back to your life and leave him to his. It's the only way. And listen: find those stashes of art I secreted in Europe. They're no good to me anymore, since I won't be around to rescue anything, and after tonight, all my debts will be paid. It's yours to do with what you want. And now I've got to go." He started striding toward the shore.

"Wait!" I called after him. "What's about to happen here?"

"All hell's about to break loose, that's what."

I scrambled after him. "You've got that right. I have a couple of hellish things on the boil, too."

We reached the shore. Ahead, the tiny islet floated on the waves while Noel stood gazing out toward a boat anchored on the ocean side of the reef.

"Noel, I've—"

"Good. They're here," he said, staring out to sea.

"Who is?" I asked, arriving breathless by his side.

"My ride. Rupert is my lift off the island."

"You called Rupert Fox?" A flicker of flashlights drew my gaze to the island. "Is that his crew on the island?"

"It took him long enough. For some reason he was all the way the hell in Tahiti."

My gut gripped. "Couldn't you have found somebody else to give you a lift?"

"I had trouble lining up a travel agent on such short notice, and Foxy has the means to make the impossible happen."

"But Rupert doesn't do anything for free. What are you paying him, Noel?"

"What do you think?" he answered without looking at me.

"The Raphael, some other piece of priceless treasure, or all of it?"

But then the sound of an engine—actually, two engines—drew our attention seaward. "A plane," I said, staring up at the spots of light growing in the night sky. "Ski plane, is my guess. That's probably my ride."

"Your ride?" Noel now stared to the left. "And there's a bloody speedboat zooming toward us."

I gripped his arm. "Could be Interpol," I said. "That's the plan I was trying to tell you about. You don't think I was just going to hang around and let everybody else's plans take over, do you?"

He shook me off. "What the hell have you done, Phoebe?"

"Whatever I did, I did for love—to save your lives, to preserve the world's art heritage," I cried. "I needed to end this thing and keep you and Toby safe!"

He swore. "That's not your choice, Phoebe!"

"I made it my choice!" I cried.

At that moment fireworks exploded overhead like a gigantic electric anemone, all pink and green with crackly silver mini bursts, while simultaneously the little island cracked and popped with its own explosions. "Right on time," I muttered, but Noel was already dashing toward the bridge.

"This is called stepping up, Noel!" I called as I scrambled after him.

🏵 21 🏵

B ut I doubted he was even listening. Too many things were happening at once. There was shouting, at least one gunshot, and another explosion. By the time we reached the center of the island, the folly was nothing but a heap of crumbling plaster with a steel door hanging askew on its frame. A high-powered lamp on the ground cast the scene into a phantasmagoric swirling stew.

"Well, this is subtle," I called out. "Whose bright idea was it to blow up the vault?"

"We did not immediately have access to the code," someone said. Evan, I thought.

Though I couldn't quite see the people through the smoke, I knew the voices.

"What is the meaning of this!" Rupert Fox, standing silhouetted before us, said to someone ahead of him shrouded in the dark. "Identify yourselves at once or we shall shoot!"

"Rupert, that is you, yes? But you should not be here." And that was Nicolina. "And do not shoot for we will then shoot back."

"Nicolina?" Rupert stepped forward. "Countess Nicolina Vanvitelli? Surely I must be hallucinating and that is not truly you. You should not be in Jamaica but Rome."

"And you should not be in Jamaica but Tahiti," Nicolina countered, stepping out of a smoky cloud. Now she could be seen holding a pistol with her black-leather-skinned legs braced apart. "I am here to rescue art and save my friend. What of you, Rupert?"

"Why, I am here to rescue art and save my friend, as well," Rupert said. "This is an impossible situation. You tricked me, Nicolina! You and Phoebe sent us to the South Pacific when the action lay here. I am deeply hurt and affronted. What is the world coming to and whatever is going on?"

"I'll tell you what's going on," I said, pushing past Noel, who immediately caught up until we were standing side by side in the dissipating haze.

"Phoebe's betrayed us," Noel said.

"I did not!" I cried, turning to him. "This is about rescue, not betrayal! I could not stand by a second longer and watch the men I love destroy themselves and take a fortune of historical art and good people down with them!"

"Phoebe?" Rupert said, looking from one of us to the other. "Tell me I am imagining this distressing, unacceptable example of falsity from one I had come to trust and respect."

"Even while you were attempting to swindle that same respected person without so much as a ping of conscience? I just did to you what you've done to me countless times," I said, knowing this was not the time for berating anybody but I couldn't stop myself.

And then a cell phone buzzed and Peaches emerged from the gloom holding a phone to her ear. "I hate to ruin dis big moment but, like, de police are hitting de main house right now. Mama, she wants to speak to you, Phoebe." She held out the phone.

Barbara shouted in my ear. "Phoebe, they are here!" she cried. "They have Tobias in custody and they be searching de house! You promised everting would be fine!"

"Everything will be fine, Barbara, I promise. My brother's a sick and dangerous man and this will get him the help he needs. Remember that all that art in his tower has been stolen and the police have the right to confiscate it. You, Lee, and all the staff have been promised immunity so just stand aside."

Meanwhile, people were moving in front of me—Noel urgently signaling to Rupert, Nicolina arguing with them both, Peaches threatening Evan, who now attempted to block the entrance to the ruined tower with his muscled self, and Max in the middle of it all trying to restore order.

"Barbara, is there a scar-faced agent there—Agent Walker?" I said urgently into the phone. "I need to speak to him now. Can you put him on for me?"

I could tell how she struggled to pull herself together and I totally identified. "Oh, I shouldn't have agreed to this! I saw him. Just wait," she said, followed by a rustling sound as if the phone had been shoved into a pocket.

Holding the phone in one hand, I plowed into the fray, yelling at my friends and enemies alike, who happened to be one and the same at that moment. "Listen, all of you! Stop arguing! The police are all over the island. They've arrested my brother—" my voice faltered but I carried on "—and...and they are now searching the main house. Whatever's going to happen here has to happen now or everyone will get arrested."

"My God, Phoebe. Is this what you call stepping up?" Noel asked.

Noel," I said, my heart cracking right down the middle, "would you take what you need and just get the hell out of here while you still can? And, Nicolina, I have to speak to Agent Walker, but after that, we can leave, too. Max, *Max?*" It was a question, a plea.

A sudden silence descended.

"It's all right, darlin'," my godfather said from the gloom. "I'm coming with you. My son has to make his own decisions and he knows his are not mine."

I could have hugged him to within an inch of his life just then but Noel strode up to his father and embraced him hard. "You take care of my Phoebe, Dad," I heard him say. "Maybe we'll be a family again someday."

"Our Phoebe's doing a damn good job of taking care of herself lately," my godfather said, his voice gruff, "and if you know what's good for you, son, you'll win her back someday. We'll be waiting."

And then Noel turned, grabbed me, squeezing me so tightly that I thought my ribs would snap along with my heart. "I'm as mad as hell at you right now, Phoebe McCabe," he whispered, "but I love you still." And he added fiercely: "Stay ahead of Foxy and deliver the items on that list I gave you, if you can, or turn the whole damn thing over to Interpol and let it thrash around in the courts. I don't care. Just don't wait for me any longer. Consider me gone."

And then he released me so quickly I stumbled backward but Nicolina steadied me. "Don't get killed," I called out to him, but he, Rupert, and Evan were already bounding toward the sea side of the islet—Evan carrying a box and another large flat package, Rupert hauling something else. There were other shapes moving in the dark, too, but at that moment I was too heartsick to move.

"This is touching, yes? To say goodbye to the man you love—very sad," Nicolina said beside me, wiping her eyes from either smoke or tears. "And yet our boat waits by the shore and the plane is not far. Seraphina has gone ahead. We must go."

"Thanks, Nicolina," I said, pulling myself together. The ruined folly still held a few metal crates and boxes inside. Let Interpol have them. From beyond the trees, I could hear a boat whirring away to sea. I wanted to die. "Max, Peaches, could you and Nicolina wait by the shore, please? I'll join you there as soon as I can."

"I'm not leaving you, Phoebe," Max said. "Do what you have to do."

"Nor am I," Nicolina said. "We are a team, yes?"

"And me, either! Are you shittin' me?" Peaches cried. "You can't just set me aside like your little minion now. I'm done with dat. Besides, I'm part of dis new team, right? You don't give me orders, we *collaborate.*" She practically spat out the word. "Besides, I've got to say goodbye to my mom and dad. I'm not going anywhere until I do."

"Wait!" I said, holding up one hand. "Peaches, if you go back to the house now, it will only complicate things horribly. Your mom—oh, shit! I forgot about your mom!" I fished the phone out of my pocket where I must have mindlessly shoved it. "Hello, Barbara?"

"It's not Barbara, but Walker. Phoebe McCabe, where are you?" a familiar voice answered. "Took you long enough to answer."

"Agent Walker, hi. I'm just dealing with some collateral damage here. Don't forget this is my brother I just handed over, and remember your assurances that he is to be kept safe even in prison, got that?"

"I intend to do everything in my power to live up to my part of the bargain." Someone was talking in the background. "What? Yes, that's important. Load that up. Ms. McCabe? My apologies. What were you saying?"

"I was saying that I'm giving you my brother and all the art he has locked away in his private quarters—that's the tower I was telling you about—in exchange for the release of his employees, who had nothing whosever to do with this debacle. They are good people who thought they were working for the management of a resort-to-be and they are innocent. Are we on the same page here or what?"

"Good Lord, he had that, too?" Walker was saying to someone. "That piece has been missing since World War II! What, hello, Ms. McCabe. I apologize again. This is an incredible hoard."

I exhaled. "Yes, it is, and now you have it all and, as I was saying, his employees are blameless."

Peaches, Max, and Nicolina were listening intently but my eyes were locked on Peaches.

"What about Noel Halloran?" Walker asked.

My gaze swerved skyward seeking a star. Ah, there. *Let it be my star, let it guide me away from what I've just done and was about to do.* "Why, isn't he there?"

"No, Ms. McCabe, he is not here. We've searched the house. Where is he?"

"I have no idea," I said truthfully, because I really didn't know *exactly* where Noel was, did I? The Caribbean was a big sea. "We had a huge blowout—understandable considering I called the police on him. It's safe to say that Noel Halloran will not be giving me his whereabouts anytime soon."

"We're fanning out over the island looking for him now. Where are you, as if I haven't asked this already?"

"Look, hate to cut this short but I've got to run, as per the other part of our agreement: I get to leave here without ever having to encounter my brother, at least not until court. You've got what you wanted. See you in London."

"Where are you?" he demanded just seconds before I powered the phone off.

I passed it back to Peaches. "Better keep it off until we're off the island. Your mom and dad will be fine, and I can only pray that ultimately Toby and Noel will be, too."

⚜ 22 ⚜

Our speedboat ride to the plane was expertly skippered by Lucas from the Washing Sands Resort; he piloted his way around those reefs with relaxed dexterity while humming a tune about coconuts and beach babes.

Max sat at the prow, staring out to sea as if seeking one last glimpse of his son, while Peaches slumped down in the plush seats staring glumly back to shore. Only Nicolina and Seraphina appeared satisfied with the night's adventure. As for the boxes and crates that filled the rest of the large luxe cabin cruiser, I hardly noticed.

I was understandably preoccupied, maybe a little battered. Though everything I'd done came from a position of strength, the last few hours had left me empty. Part of me thought I would die from the pain of it all.

About twenty minutes later, we loaded ourselves onto the ski plane. The fact that Fabio and Captain Octavio were manning the skies once again hardly registered. Had Amelia Earhart dropped in to pilot us back to Rome, I wouldn't have batted an eyelash—too bruised, too stunned by what I had just done.

We buckled in and took off, a silent group still processing events. Nobody had clean hands.

JANE THORNLEY

Somewhere on the mainland, we switched planes and took off again, still with Captain Octavio at the helm, though Seraphina relieved him as co-pilot this time. So what if Nicolina's assistant had her cross-Atlantic pilot's license, too? Big deal.

We slept. Occasionally, I'd awaken to that surreal mechanical airplane hum and the sight of my friends in various sleeping states around the dimmed cabin. Fabio always seemed to be on a trip-wire state to feed and water anybody who so much as twitched.

"Phoebe, are you awake?" he asked, slipping in beside me when I'd opened my eyes long enough to realize I had to pee.

"No, it only looks that way," I replied, sitting up.

"Here's a mug of hot tea I made with some soul-soothing herbs I thought you might need, given everything that's just happened."

I took the mug and sipped. "Thanks. Hell knows I need soul-soothing."

"I just want you to know that Otty and I are totally with you on this new venture. I'm just so excited! I mean, to be part of this team is really, really big, and sooo scrumptious."

"It is?"

"Oh, yes, absolutely."

"What team?"

He whisked a hand across his blond faux-hawk and gave me a playful nudge. "Kidding, right?" Luckily I had set down my tea by then. "You know, all of us returning rare art to its rightful owners. I mean, that's important, and to be part of something that aids humanity, how perfect is that? Like, I always wanted to do something grand but now it's like my dreams have come true—a worthy mission, at last. And I just adore art."

I stared unfocused at Peaches's blanket-wrapped body splayed out on the pulldown bed opposite mine. One long leg dangled from the blankets as she moaned in her sleep. "You do?"

"Oh, yes, totally, especially Italian art—got to love those Italians, and I do, though I'm bound to only one at the moment." And he laughed. "Anyways, Phoebe, I just wanted you to know that Captain Otty and I are totally on board."

"Good." Though I couldn't recall using the term *on board* that didn't

184

involve boats or planes. Maybe he was confused. I knew I was. Baffled, I just sat for a moment as Fabio dashed off to fetch a cup of espresso for Nicolina. The cabin's occupants were coming to life.

A few minutes later, I went off to the washroom, and on the return trip, Nicolina beckoned for me to join her.

"Hi, Nicolina," I said, landing next to her. "I really haven't had a chance to thank you properly since, well, since..."

She waved away the notion. "There is no need to thank me. I said I help and so I help, and now we take these things back to Italy."

"What things?"

"In the cargo," she said, "and there and there."

I focused on the crates and boxes she indicated wedged between the spare seats. Slowly, realization dawned. "From the vault?"

"From the vault, yes. We took as much as we could, but Rupert, he took other things. We struggled together, yes, but nobody could hurt the other for we are all friends, right? In the end, we share. I do not know what is in the boxes but we will find out in Rome and then return them to their owners."

"In other words," Max said, suddenly standing above us, "we will finish off what Noel initially started."

"We will become the new Robin Hoods," Nicolina said, "though we will not steal and I do not like Maid Marian—too, how do you say? Dull! Yes, too dull. We will be the band of merry people and will not steal. Unless absolutely necessary," she added, as if more to herself than to anyone else. "But we must restore, yes, restore, the way you restored my heritage—and my *nonna*—to me."

I shook my head, more to realign my thoughts than because I disagreed. I was still trying to kick-start my brain. "But why not turn it all over to Interpol?"

"Interpol!" Nicolina's hands flew up. "They will only go to tribunals and debate and debate—"

"Get bogged down in legal shenanigans," Max added.

"Legal shenanigans, yes!"

"Plus, they have a ton of art in Toby's quarters to deal with already, don't they?" Max asked. "That lot will keep Agent Walker's crew busy for months."

My gaze landed on my carpetbag across the aisle where I'd transcribed Noel's coded list into stitches. Now if I could just recall them when I needed to. A tingle of possibility hit my spine. I rubbed my temples. "Wait, wait. This is a huge enterprise you're talking about—huge! Restoring art to its rightful owners without Interpol? That's borderline illegal, not like that's anything new among present company."

"Speak for yourself, Phoebe." That was Peaches, now sitting up on her fold-down bed. "I just shoot at people, remember?"

"And build things," I told her. "You're actually quite a dynamo." She grinned and saluted me.

"Back to the illegal business," Max interjected, "I think it's safe to say you've won Agent Walker's respect, Phoebe. I just bet he'd be interested in collaborating with you—with us—in some capacity. You've already proved yourself in his eyes."

"Yeah, while just taking off with more stolen loot," I said, pointing to one of the crates. "How do we explain those?"

Nicolina fixed me with her luminous eyes. "We say nothing. Who will know? And in Rome, I do the talking."

"You mean like this?" I rubbed my fingers together.

"Whatever works." She smiled.

"Do we even know what's in those?" I asked, staring at the crates again.

Nicolina shrugged. "Something important, yes? Maybe the Raphael."

"Or one of them." I leaned forward, noting for the first time how my designer clothes were filthy and shredded and how little I cared. "Toby was busy mass-producing them but Noel would have told Foxy exactly where the true one was hidden." And then it hit me again...the enormity of what I'd done. "Oh, Toby, he'll never forgive me, and Noel —" I was just seconds away from losing it again.

Max put a hand on my shoulder while Nicolina grasped my hand. "It is hard, I know," she said, "to go against those we love." She studied me earnestly. "It was not easy for me to go against my grandpapa or my brother, but it was something I had to do, as did you. We must do what we believe is right, the honorable thing, or we cannot—" she struggled for the right word "—or we cannot breathe, yes, *breathe*. For this, you must be strong."

"But I sent my brother to jail!" I wailed. "I betrayed the man I loved!"

"Maybe they betrayed you first," Max said quietly. "They made their choices and those choices don't have to be yours any longer. The two of us have allowed ourselves to be jerked around by the repercussions of their actions for years."

"But now we set our own terms," I said, straightening. "We're stepping up. Where would we be based?"

"In Rome," answered Nicolina.

"In London," said Max.

I held up my hand. "In both Rome and London—got it."

"And we're nominating you as leader," Max added.

"Since when?" I looked up at him.

"Since now. We're about to take a vote," Nicolina told me.

"We are? Why does it sound like everybody knows about this except me?"

"You've been kind of preoccupied, darlin', and Nicolina and I had a chance to talk. So," and Max called out: "I hereby nominate Phoebe McCabe as leader. All those in agreement say, 'Aye.'"

The "ayes" were unanimous. Amid clapping and whooping, I got to my feet. "Thank you, friends. To say that I am honored is too flimsy a word, but I am. Let's go off and do the job the way it should have been done in the first place. Let's take the plunge!"

"Don't use that word, Phoebe," Fabio called. "Not while we're on a plane, please! But we'll be arriving in Rome in about twenty minutes," Fabio called as he rolled a breakfast wagon down the aisle. "Back to your seats now and buckle up now. We may be landing soon, but the ride has just begun!

THE END

JOIN MY NEWSLETTER

Join my newsletter on my web page at janethornley.com to stay up to date on all the creative things I get up to as well as my latest books, workshops, and dreams.

ABOUT THE AUTHOR

JANE THORNLEY is an author of mystery and suspense. Though both a writer and a designer, Jane has lived many lives including teacher, school principal, superintendent of schools, and librarian. She also once dabbled in software design and lead tour groups around the world.

These days, Jane lives a very dull life. Luckily her imagination makes to for it.

This is the fifth book in JANE's *Crime by Design Series*.

ALSO BY JANE THORNLEY

Crime by Design Boxed Set Books 1-3
Crime by Design Book 1: Rogue Wave
Crime by Design Book 2: Warp in the Weave
Crime by Design Book 3: Beautiful Survivor
Crime by Design Book 4: The Greater of Two Evils
Crime by Design Book 5: The Plunge

None of the Above Series Book 1: Downside Up

Made in the USA
Coppell, TX
07 February 2023

12386942R00114